The Doll's Bad News

(originally published as *Twelve Chinks and a Woman*)

A Panther Book

A Panther Book

First published in Great Britain by Jarrolds Publishers (London) Limited (as *Twelve Chinks and a Woman*) 1941. Panther edition published 1970.

Made and printed in Great Britain by C. Nicholls & Company Ltd., The Philips Park Press, Manchester, and published by Panther Books, 3 Upper James Street, London, W.1.

The Doll's Bad News

Chapter One

Fenner opened one eye as Paula Dolan put some elegant curves and her fluffy head round his office door. He regarded her vaguely, and then settled himself more comfortably. His large feet rested on the snowy blotting-pad, and the swivelled desk-chair inclined perilously at an angle of 45°. He said sleepily, 'Run away, Dizzy, I'll play with you later. Right now I'm thinking.'

Some more curves filtered through the half-open door, and Paula came to the desk. 'Wake up, Morpheus,' she said; 'you've got a client.'

Fenner groaned. 'Tell him to go away. Tell him we've gone outta business. I gotta catch up some sleep sometimes, haven't I?'

'What's your bed for?' Paula said impatiently.

'Don't ask questions like that,' Fenner mumbled, settling himself further down in the chair.

'Snap out of it, Dave,' Paula pleaded; 'there's a passion flower waiting outside, and she looks as if she's got a load of grief to share with you.'

Fenner opened an eye again. 'What's she like?' he asked. 'Maybe she's collecting for some charity.'

Paula sat on the edge of the desk. 'Sometimes I wonder why you keep that plate on your door. Don't you want to do business?'

Fenner shook his head. 'Not if I can help it,' he said. 'We're in the dough, ain't we? Let's take it easy.'

'You're passing up something pretty good. Still, if that's the way you feel . . .' Paula slid off the desk.

'Hey, wait a minute.' Fenner sat up and pushed his hat off his eyes. 'Is she really a passion flower?'

Paula nodded. 'I guess she's in trouble, Dave.'

'Okay, okay, send her in, send her in.'

Paula opened the door. She said, 'Will you come in?'

A voice said, 'Thank you,' and a young woman came in. She walked slowly past Paula, looking at Fenner with large, smoky-blue eyes.

She was a shade taller than average, and pliantly slender. Her legs were long, her hands and feet narrow, and her body was very erect. Her hair, curling under her prim little hat, was raven black. She wore a severe two-piece costume, and she looked very young and very scared.

Paula gave her an encouraging smile and went out, shutting the door quietly behind her.

Fenner took his feet off the desk and stood up. 'Sit down,' he said, 'and tell me what I can do for you.' He indicated the armchair by his desk.

She shook her head. 'I'd rather stand,' she said breathlessly. 'I may not be here very long.'

Fenner sat down again. 'You can do just what you like here,' he said soothingly. 'This place is anyone's home.'

They remained looking at each other for a long minute. Then Fenner said, 'You know you'd better sit down. You've got a lot to tell me, an' you look tired.'

He could see she wasn't scared of him, she was scared of something that he didn't know anything about. Her eyes were uneasy, and she held her high-breasted body as though she was ready to jump for the door.

Again she shook her head. 'I want you to find my sister,' she said breathlessly. 'I'm so worried about my sister. What will it cost? I mean, what are your fees?'

Fenner squinted at the inkwell by his hand. 'Suppose you don't worry your head about the cost. Just relax an' tell me all about it,' he said. 'Tell me who you are for a start.'

The telephone jangled at his elbow. The effect on the girl was startling. She took two quick graceful steps away from the 'phone, and her eyes went cloudy and big.

Fenner grinned at her. 'I guess I get the same way,' he said quietly, pulling the receiver towards him. 'When I fall asleep an' the bell goes off, I guess it scares the shirt right off my back.'

She stood very tense by the door, watching him.

Fenner said, 'Excuse me a moment,' as he took off the receiver. 'Yeah?' he said.

There was a lot of crackling on the line. Then a man said with a very liquid accent: 'Fenner?'

'Yeah.'

'Any moment now, Fenner, a girl is going to call in and see you. I want you to hold her until I get round to your office. I'm on my way now. Do you understand?'

Fenner let his eyes fall on the girl, and he smiled at her reassuringly. 'I don't get it,' he said to the telephone.

'Well, listen, only get this right. A girl will come and see you about a story of her missing sister. Well, hold her for me. She's suffering from delusions. She got away from an asylum yesterday, and I know she's heading for your office. Just hold her for me.'

Fenner pushed his hat on to the bridge of his nose. 'Who in hell are you?' he said.

There was more crackling on the wire. 'I'll explain when I get around. I'm coming right away. Your fee will be paid on a generous scale if you do this.'

Fenner said, 'Okay, you come on up.'

The girl said, 'Did he say I was crazy?' The hand that wasn't holding her bag fluttered up and down the seam of her skirt.

Fenner put the receiver on its prong. He nodded shortly.

She shut her eyes for a second, then her lids rolled back like a doll's that has been sat up suddenly. She said desperately, 'It's so difficult not to believe him.' Then she put her bag on the desk, stripped off her gloves and hastily pulled off her coat. Fenner sat quite still, his hand on the telephone, watching her. She gave a little sob and then, with trembling fingers, she began to undo her shirt blouse.

Fenner shifted. 'You don't have to do this,' he said uneasily. 'I'm interested in your case without any act.'

Once again she caught her breath in a sob and turned her back on him. She pulled the blouse off. Fenner's hand strayed to the bell. Maybe this dame was nutty, and was going to hold him up for assault. Then he stiffened and took his hand away. Her back showed distinct, livid bruises, startlingly vivid against her white skin. Some of them were in the shape of finger-prints. She put on the blouse again, fastened the buttons, and then put on her coat. Then she turned round and looked at Fenner with her eyes bigger than ever.

'Now do you believe I'm in trouble?' she said.

Fenner shook his head. 'You didn't have to do that,' he said. 'You came to me for help. Okay, why look further? You don't have to be scared.'

She stood there, torturing her lower lip with her glistening teeth. Then she opened her bag and took out a roll of notes. She put them on the desk. 'Will that do as a retainer?' she said.

Fenner touched the roll with a thick finger. Without actually counting the money he couldn't be sure, but he was willing to bet that there was at least six grand in that roll. He got up swiftly, picked up the roll, and stepped to the door. 'Stay here,' he said, and went outside into the outer office.

Paula was sitting at the typewriter, her hands in her lap and her eyes expectant.

Fenner said, 'Grab your hat quick, an' take this baby to the Baltimore Hotel. Get her a room there and tell her to lock herself in. Take this roll and when you've fixed her, sock it in the bank. Find out all you can about her. Tell her I'll look after her. Give her the you're-in-good-hands dope. Feed her a good line of syrup. She's got the jitters; she's in trouble and she's still young enough to need a mother.'

He went back to the office. 'What's your name?' he said.

The girl beat her hands together. 'Do get me away from here,' she said.

Fenner put his hand on her arm. 'I'm sending you out with my secretary. She'll look after you. There's a guy on his way up who's interested in you. I'll take care of him. What's your name?'

'Marian Daley,' she said. Then she swallowed and went on hurriedly: 'Where shall I go?'

Paula came in, pulling on her gloves. Fenner nodded. 'Go with Miss Dolan,' he said. 'Go down the back way. You'll be okay now. Don't get scared any more.'

Marian Daley gave him a timid little smile. 'I'm glad I came to you,' she said. 'You see, I'm in a lot of trouble. It's my sister as well. What can she want with twelve Chinese?'

Fenner blew out his cheeks. 'Search me,' he said, leading her to the door. 'Maybe she likes Chinamen. Some people do, you know. Just take it easy until I see you tonight.'

He stepped into the passage and watched them walk to the elevator. When the cage shot out of sight he wandered back into the office. He shut the door softly behind him and went over to his desk. He opened the top drawer and took out a .38 police special. He was playing hunches. He put the gun inside his coat and sat down behind the desk. He put his feet up again and shut his eyes.

He sat like that for ten minutes or so, his mind busy with theories. Three things intrigued him: The six thousand dollars, the bruises on the girl's back and the twelve Chinese. Why all that dough as a retainer? Why didn't she just tell him that someone had bruised her instead of stripping? Why tell him *twelve* Chinese? Why not just say, "What did she want with Chinese"?

Why twelve? He shifted in his seat. Then there was the guy on the 'phone. Was she fresh from a nut farm after all? He doubted it. She had been badly scared, but she was normal enough. He opened his eyes and glanced at the small chromium clock on his desk. She had been gone twelve minutes. How long would this guy take to come up?

As he was thinking, he became aware that he was not concentrating as he should. Half his mind was listening to someone whistling outside in the corridor. He moved irritably and brought his mind back to the immediate problem. Who was Marian Daley? Obiously she was a rich girl of the upper crust. Her clothes must have cost a nice pile of dough. He wished the guy outside would stop whistling. What was the tune, anyway? He listened. Then very softly he began to hum the mournful strains of *Chloe* with the whistler.

The haunting tune held him, and he stopped humming and listened to the fluting sound, beating out the time with his index finger on the back of his hand. Then he suddenly felt a little chilled. Whoever was whistling was not moving. The low penetrating sound kept at the same degree of loudness, as if the whistler was standing outside his door, whistling to him.

Fenner took his feet off his desk very softly and eased the chair away gently. The mournful tune continued. He put his hand inside his coat and felt the butt of the .38. Although there was only one entrance to his office, and that was through the outer office, he had an exit in his own office, which he kept locked. This door led to the back entrance of the block. It was from outside this exit that the whistling was coming.

He walked to the door and softly turned the key in the lock, carefully keeping his shadow from falling on the frosted panel. As he eased the door handle and gently began to open the door, the whistling stopped abruptly. He stepped out into the corridor and looked up and down. There was no one about. Moving fast, he went to the head of the staircase and looked down into the well. The place was deserted. Turning, he walked the length of the corridor and looked down the well of the other flight of stairs. Still nothing to see.

Pushing his hat on to the bridge of his nose, he stood listening. Faintly, he could hear the roar of the traffic floating up from the street, the whine of the elevators as they raced between floors, and the persistent ticking of the big clock above his head. He walked slowly back to his office and stood in the open doorway, his nerves a little tense. As he went in and shut the door the whistling started again.

His eyes went very bleak and he walked into the outer office, the .38 in his hand. He stopped just in the doorway and grunted. A small man in a black shabby suit sat hunched up in one of the padded chairs reserved for visitors. His hat was pulled so far down that Fenner could not see his face. Fenner knew by just looking at him that he was dead. He put the gun into his hip pocket and moved nearer. He looked at the small yellow bony hands that rested limply in the man's lap. Then he leant forward and pulled the hat off the man's head.

He was not a pleasant sight. He was a Chinese all right. Someone had cut his throat, starting just under his right ear and going in a neat half-circle to his left ear. The wound had been stitched up neatly, but just the same, the Chinese was quite a nightmare to see.

Fenner blotted his face with his handkerchief. 'Quite a day,' he said softly.

As he stood, wondering what the hell to do next, the telephone began to ring. He went over to the extension, shoved the plug in and picked up the receiver.

Paula sounded excited. 'She's gone, Dave,' she said. 'We got as far as the Baltimore and then she vanished.'

Fenner blew out his cheeks. 'You mean someone snatched her?'

'No. She just took a runout on me. I was fixing up her room at the desk, turned my head, saw her beating it for the exit, and by the time I got into the street she'd gone.'

'What about the dough?' Fenner said. 'That gone too?'

'That's safe enough. Right now that's in the bank. But what am I going to do? Shall I come on back?'

Fenner looked at the Chinese. 'Hang around the Baltimore and buy yourself a lunch. I'll come on out when I'm through. Right now I've got a client.'

'But, Dave, what about the girl? Hadn't you better come now?'

Fenner was inclined to be impatient. 'I'm runnin' this office,' he said shortly. 'Every minute I keep this guy waitin' he gets colder and colder, an' believe me, it ain't with rage.' He dropped the receiver into its cradle and straightened up. He looked at the Chinese unemotionally. 'Well, come on, Percy,' he said. 'You an' I gotta take a walk.'

Paula sat in the Baltimore lounge until after three o'clock. She had worked herself up to a severe tension when, at quarter-past three, Fenner came across the lounge fast, his eyebrows meeting in a heavy frown of concentration and his eyes hard and frosty. He said, pausing just long enough to pick up her coat lying on a vacant chair beside her, 'Come on, baby, I wantta talk to you.'

Paula followed him into the cocktail lounge, which was almost empty. Fenner led her to a table at the far end of the room, opposite the entrance. He took some care to pull the table away from the wall, so that he could sit facing the swing-doors.

'Are you usin' booze as perfume these days,' he said, sitting down, 'or do you think we can get some hard liquor in this joint?'

'That's a nice crack,' Paula said; 'what else can a girl do in a place like this? I've only had three martinis. What's the idea? I've been sitting on my tail for three hours now.'

Fenner beckoned to a waiter. 'Don't say tail. It's vulgar.' He ordered two double Scotches and some ginger-ale. He sat with his back turned to Paula and watched the waiter order the drinks and bring them all the way back. When the waiter had set them down he reached out and poured one of the doubles into the other glass, filled the empty glass half full of ginger-ale and pushed it over to Paula. 'You gotta watch your complexion, Dizzy,' he said, and poured half the neat Scotch down his throat.

Paula sighed. 'Well, come on,' she said impatiently, 'let me in on the ground floor. I've been out of circulation for three hours.'

Fenner lit a cigarette and leant back in his chair. 'You're quite sure Miss Daley walked out on you without any persuasion?'

Paula nodded. 'It was like I told you. I went up to the desk and started making arrangements for a room. She was standing behind me. I took off my glove to sign the book and I felt sort of lonely. I looked round and there she was drifting into the street. She was on her own and moving fast. By the time I'd got through the revolving door she'd gone. I tell you, Dave, I got a nasty shock. What was worrying me more than anything was I'd got all that money on me. I guess you were nuts to have given it to me."

Fenner grinned unpleasantly. 'You don't know just how smart I was, baby,' he said. 'I guess I did myself a nice turn sending you out with that dough. Anyway, go on.'

'I went back to the hotel, asked for an envelope, put the money in and gave it to the cashier to hold. Then I shot out into the street and had a look round; didn't get anywhere, so I 'phoned you.'

Fenner nodded. 'Okay. If you're sure she ran out without some guy pushin' her to it, we'll let it ride for a moment.'

Paula said, 'I'm positive!'

'Now let me tell you somethin'. There's somethin' mighty phoney about this business. Someone planted a dead Chink in the outer office after you'd gone, and tipped the cops.'

Paula sat up. 'A dead Chink?'

Fenner smiled mirthlessly. 'Yeah. This Chink had a slit in his throat and had been dead some time. He would want some explainin' away. Soon as I saw him, I asked myself why. Either that guy was left as a warnin' or else a plant. I wasn't takin' any chances, so I moved him out quick and tossed him in an empty office at the end of the corridor. Well, I was right. It was a plant. I hadn't got back more than a few minutes before three tough bulls bust in. They were lookin' for that Chink, and, believe me, it took all I had not to laugh in their faces.'

'But why?' Paula asked, her eyes very wide.

'Suppose they found him there? I should have been taken down to the station and held. That's what was wanted. To get me out of the way long enough to catch up with this Daley dame. These bulls softened up a lot when they found nothin' to holler about, but they searched the two offices. I had my fingers crossed. If they had found that six grand it might have taken a little explainin' away.'

Paula said, 'But what's all this mean?'

'Search me. It just amuses me; but it don't mean anythin' yet. What did you get out of Miss Daley?'

Paula shook her head. 'She just wasn't talkin'. I asked her the usual line for our records, but she said she would only talk to you.'

Fenner finished his Scotch and stubbed out his cigarette. 'Investigation seems about to peter out,' he said. 'We're six grand to the good an' no work to do for it.'

'But you won't sit around doin' nothing?'

'Why not? She paid me the dough, didn't she? Then when I fix it so she can talk in comfort she blows. Why should I worry? When she wants more advice she'll contact me.'

An elderly man with a lean face, all nose and chin, came into the lounge and sat down a few tables from them. Paula looked at him curiously. She thought by the look of his eyes he'd been weeping. She wondered why. Fenner broke into her thoughts.

'What did you think of this Daley dame?' he said abruptly.

Paula knew what he wanted. 'She was educated. Her clothes were class and cost plenty. She was scared about something. I could guess at her age, but I'd most likely make a mistake. I'd say twenty-four. I might be six years out either way. If she was anything but a good girl, she was a good actress. Her make-up was mild and she'd been living in the sun a lot. She was modest –"

Fenner nodded his head. 'I was waiting for that. Sure, she was the modest type. Then why should she take off her clothes to show me her bruises?'

Paula put her glass down and stared at him. 'This is a new one,' she said.

'Oh, I'll get round to everythin' in time.' Fenner waved his glass at the waiter. 'You don't know about the guy who 'phoned me while I was talkin' to her an' told me she was nuts. That's when she went into the strip-tease. That's what's gettin' me. It don't line up with her type. She just took off her coat and blouse and stood around the office in her brassière. It don't add up.'

'Someone had bruised her?'

'I'll say someone had bruised her. The marks on her back looked like they were painted on, they were so vivid.'

Paula thought for a moment. 'Maybe she was scared that you'd think she was crazy and, by showing you that, you'd see she was in a jam.'

Fenner nodded. 'It might go like that, but I don't like it.'

While the waiter was fixing him another drink, Paula glanced at the elderly man again. She said to Fenner, 'Don't look now, but there's a man over there taking a great interest in you.'

'What of it?' Fenner said impatiently. 'Maybe he likes my face.'

'It couldn't be that. I guess he thinks you're made up for the films.'

The elderly man got up abruptly and came over. He stood uncertain, and he looked so sad that Paula gave him an encouraging smile. He addressed himself to Fenner.

'You'll excuse me,' he said, 'but are you Mr. Fenner?'

'That's right,' Fenner said without any enthusiasm.

'My name's Lindsay. Andrew Lindsay. I wanted your help.'

Fenner shifted restlessly. 'I'm glad to know you, Mr. Lindsay,' he said, 'but I couldn't be any help to you.'

Lindsay looked disconcerted. His eyes wandered to Paula and then back to Fenner.

'Won't you sit down, Mr. Lindsay?' Paula said.

Fenner shot her a hard look, but Paula wouldn't see it.

Lindsay hesitated and then sat down.

Paula went on with a show of manners that almost embarrassed Fenner. 'Mr. Fenner's a very busy man, but I've never known him to turn down anyone who was in trouble.'

Fenner thought, 'This little smartie's goin' to get smacked when we're alone.' He nodded his head at Lindsay because he had to. 'Sure,' he said. 'What's bitin' you?'

'Mr. Fenner, I've read about how you found the Blandish girl when she was kidnapped. I'm in the same trouble. My little girl disappeared yesterday.' Two tears ran down his thin face. Fenner shifted his eyes. 'Mr. Fenner, I'm asking you· to help find her. She was all I had, and God knows what has become of her.'

Fenner finished his whisky and put the glass down on the table with a click. 'You've told the police?' he said abruptly.

Lindsay nodded.

'Kidnappin' is a Federal offence. I can't do better'n the F.B.I. You must be patient. They'll turn her up.'

'But, Mr. Fenner –'

Fenner shook his head. He got to his feet. 'I'm sorry, but I can't get round to it.'

Lindsay's face puckered like a disappointed child's. He put out his hand and held on to Fenner's sleeve.

'Mr. Fenner, do this for me. You won't regret it. You can charge what you like. You can find my little girl sooner than anyone. I know you can. Mr. Fenner, I beg you to do this.'

Fenner's eyes were chips of ice. He took Lindsay's hand off his arm gently but firmly. 'Listen,' he said. 'I'm my own boss; I don't work for anyone. If I want to take an assignment, I take it. If I don't, I turn it down. Right now, I've got something that's giving me an itch. I'm sorry your kid's got herself into trouble, but I can't do anythin' about it. The F.B.I. is big enough to take care of your daughter and hundreds of other guys' daughters. I'm sorry, but I'm not doing it.'

He jerked his head at Paula and walked out of the lounge. Lindsay dropped his hands helplessly, and began to cry very quietly. Paula patted his arm. Then she got up and went out of the lounge. Fenner was standing waiting for her. He said savagely, as she walked up.

'You must start crimpin'. What the hell do you think we're runnin' – a dog's home?'

Paula gave him a mean look. 'That old guy's lost his daughter; doesn't that mean anything to you?'

'It means a pain in the neck to me, that's all.' Fenner snapped. 'Come on back to the office – we've got work to do.'

'There are times when I think you're cute,' Paula said bitterly, moving towards the reception hall. 'But right now I'd swop you for a lead nickel and a bad smell.'

A tall young man uncurled himself from one of the big lounges and stepped up to Fenner. 'I'm Grosset of the D.A.'s office. I want to talk to you.'

Fenner grunted. 'I'm busy right now, pal,' he said. 'Call round at my office tomorrow some time, when I'm out.'

Grosset apologetically indicated two big cops in plain clothes who stood right in Fenner's exit. 'We can talk here, or at my office,' he said primly.

Fenner grinned. 'A hold-up? Okay, let's talk here, and quick.'

Paula said, 'I've forgotten something. I'll be right back.' She left them and went back into the cocktail lounge. Lindsay was still sitting there. She sat down beside him. 'You mustn't feel that Mr. Fenner means to be unkind,' she said softly. 'He's got a case that's worrying him. He gets like that. He doesn't mean anything.'

Lindsay raised his head and looked at her. 'I guess I shouldn't have asked him,' he said helplessly; 'but my little girl means a lot to me.'

Paula opened her bag and took out a flat note-book. 'Give me the facts,' she said. 'I can't promise anything, but I might be able to persuade him.'

The heavy eyes lit up a little hopefully. 'I can do that,' he said huskily. 'What facts do you want?'

In the lounge outside, Fenner followed Grosset to a quiet corner and sat down with him. He was very watchful and distrusting.

Grosset was smooth, just a shade too smooth. He flicked open a thin gold cigarette-case and offered it to Fenner. He then lit the two cigarettes with a gold lighter.

Fenner said dryly, 'You guys live well.'

Grosset said, 'I don't think we've run into you before.' He crossed his legs, showing black-and-white check socks. 'I've checked your licence. You were the guy who made so much money out of the Blandish kidnapping case. That was when you were a down-at-heel investigator new on the job. You got a lucky break and you pulled out of Kansas and put up a plate here. That's right, isn't it?'

Fenner forced a long stream of smoke down his nostrils. 'You're tellin' the story,' he said; 'you've got it right up to now.'

Grosset looked wise. 'You've been in New York six months. You don't seem to have done much in that time.'

Fenner yawned. 'I pick an' choose,' he said indifferently.

'We got a pretty hot tip about you this morning.'

Fenner sneered pleasantly. 'Yeah? So hot you sent some bulls out to haul me in and they went away with fleas in their ears.'

Grosset smiled. 'Since then, we've looked over the block,' he said. 'We've found a murdered Chinaman in an empty office near yours.'

Fenner raised his eyebrows. 'What you squawking about? Want me to find who killed him for you?'

'The tip we got this morning was about a dead Chinaman who was to be found in your office.'

'Ain't that sad? What happened? Did they plant him in the wrong room?'

Grosset dropped his cigarette butt into the ash-tray.

'Listen, Fenner, you and I don't have to fight. I'll put my cards on the table. That Chink had been dead thirty-six hours. The tip was clumsy and we guessed it was a plant, but we had to look into it. Well, we're interested in this Chinaman. We want to get a line on him. Suppose you give us your angle of this?'

Fenner scratched his nose.

'Brother,' he said, 'I feel like I want to beat a drum in the Salvation Army after that speech. If I knew a thing about it, I'd tell you. If that Chink meant anything to me I'd give it to you fast, but he doesn't. I've never had a Chink in my office. I've never set eyes on your dead Chink, and I hope to God I never will.'

Grosset looked at him thoughtfully. 'I've heard you were like that,' he said gloomily. 'You like to run on your own and then turn the whole thing over to us after you've got it sewn up. All right, if that's the way you want to play it, go ahead. If we can help you, we will, but if you get into trouble we'll crack down on you so hard you'll think the Empire State building is on your neck.'

Fenner grinned and got to his feet. 'All set?' he said. 'If you're through, I got some work to do.'

Grosset nodded. 'Hang around, Fenner; I'll be seeing you again before long.' He jerked his head at his two watch-dogs, and the three of them walked out of the lobby.

Paula came out of the cocktail lounge and caught up with Fenner as he moved to the exit. He said, 'Where have *you* been?'

'Listen, Dave,' she said, 'I've been talking to Mr. Lindsay. I've got a record of what's been happening to his daughter. Why don't you have a look at it?'

Fenner regarded her with a cold eye. 'You wearin' your armour-platin'?''

'What's it to you what I'm wearing?'

'Only when I get you back to the office I'm goin' to apply somethin' pretty hard to it, an', baby, you'll keep perpendicular for a fortnight after I'm through with you. And listen, not another word about Lindsay and his daughter. I ain't interested, I've never been interested, and I never will be interested. I've got enough on my mind to last me a lifetime.'

'Considering the size of your mind, it doesn't surprise me,' Paula said coldly, and followed him out into the street.

Back in his office, Fenner went straight to his desk and sat down. He lit a cigarette and shouted to Paula. 'Come on in, Dizzy.'

Paula slid through the door and sat down at his elbow, her pencil poised over her note-book. Fenner shook his head. 'I ain't dictating,' he said. 'I want you to keep me company.'

Paula folded her hands in her lap. 'Okay,' she said. 'I'll be your stooge.'

Fenner brooded. 'Maybe I could get an angle if I turned that money over to the cops to track up. I should be lettin' 'em in if I did. Grosset is worried about the Chink. He'll keep his eye on me. Anythin' I do is goin' to be shared with that bright boy.'

'Why not? He might find the girl for you if you let him have a chance.'

Fenner shook his head. 'I'm still playin' hunches,' he said. 'Somethin' tells me that the cops are best outta this.'

Paula glanced at the clock. It was getting on to five. 'I've got some work to do,' she said. 'You won't get anywhere right now.'

Fenner said impatiently, 'Stick around, stick around. Ain't you on my pay-roll no more?'

Paula settled herself more comfortably. When he was like this she knew it was better to let him have his way.

'Unless this dame contacts me, the case will peter out. I've got no lead to go on. I don't know who she is. She might come from anywhere. All I know is she's got a sister who's interested in twelve Chinamen. If the dead Chink was one of them, there are only eleven for her to be interested in now. Why did she give me all that dough, and then take it on the lam?'

'Suppose she saw someone she knew, got scared, and lost her head?' Paula put in softly.

Fenner thought this one over. 'Did you see anyone who might have given her a scare?'

Paula shook her head. 'You know what the Baltimore lobby's like that time of day.'

'It's an idea.' Fenner got up and began walking up and down the gaily patterned carpet. 'If that's how it went, then we've gotta stick around this telephone for her to ring back. Maybe she won't ring, but if she does, I want to know about it quick.'

Paula groaned.

'Yeah, I guess you'd better run home, pack a bag an' move in. You can sleep on the lounge.'

Paula got to her feet. 'You go home and sleep in your nice warm bed, I take it?'

'Never mind what I do. I'll let you know where you can get me.'

Paula put on her hat and coat. 'If the office downstairs knows that I'm sleepin' here, they'll begin to think things.'

'That's all right. They know I'm particular. It won't blow out into a scandal.'

Paula swept out, shutting the door with a firm click behind her. Fenner grinned and grabbed the telephone. He dialled a number.

'D.A. office? Give me Grosset. Tell him Fenner wants him.'

Grosset came through after a barrage of crackles. 'Hello, Fenner. You changed your mind and want to talk?'

Fenner grinned into the receiver.

'Not just yet, pal,' he said. 'I want you to talk instead. This Chink you found lyin' around. Did you find anythin' on him that might help?'

Grosset laughed. 'By God, Fenner! You've got a nerve. You don't expect information from me, do you?'

Fenner said seriously: 'Listen, Grosset, this case hasn't started to break yet. I got a hunch that when it does, someone's goin' to yell murder. I want to stop it before it starts.'

'I warn you, Fenner, if you're holding back anything it's going to be just too bad for you. If something happens that I could've stopped, and I find you knew about it, I'm going to ride you.'

Fenner shifted in his chair.

'Skip it, Jughead,' he said impatiently. 'You know I'm in my rights to keep my client covered. If you like to play ball an' give me the information, I'll turn it back to you with interest if I think trouble's startin'. How's that?'

'You're a smooth bird,' Grosset said doubtfully. 'Still, what I know won't be much good. We found nothing.'

'How did they get him in?'

'That wasn't so difficult. They brought him in a big laundry basket, up the trade entrance, and unpacked him in an empty office before shooting him into your room.'

'Don't try to pull that one,' Fenner said. 'They didn't bring him to me. They left him in the empty office.'

Grosset made a noise like tearing calico.

'Did anyone see the guys who brought him?'

'No.'

'Well, thanks, pal. I'll do the same for you one day. Nothin' else? Nothin' that seemed odd to you?'

'Well, no, I don't think so. Someone had cut his throat and sewn it up for him – that's odd, I suppose.'

'Yeah, but I could see that. Nothing else, huh?'

'I guess not.'

Fenner hung the receiver on its prong. He sat staring at the telephone for several minutes, his face blank, and a puzzled look clouding his eyes.

Paula, coming back a couple of hours later, found him sitting slouched in his chair, his feet on the desk, tobacco ash all over his coat, and the same puzzled look in his eyes.

She put a small suit-case on the lounge and took off her hat and coat. 'Anything break?'

Fenner shook his head. 'If it wasn't for that dead Chink, I'd write it off as easy money. Those guys wouldn't have risked carting the stiff all the way up to my office unless they were mighty anxious to get me out of the way.'

Paula opened her case and took out a book. 'I've had my dinner,' she said, sitting in the padded chair near the desk. 'I'm all set. If you want to be excused, you can go.'

Fenner nodded. He got up and brushed himself down. 'Okay,' he said. 'I'll be back in a little while. If she rings, tell her I want to see her bad. Get her address and still feed her syrup. I want to get close to that dame.'

'I was afraid of that,' Paula murmured, but Fenner went to the door without hearing her.

Just outside, two men, dressed in black suits, stood shoulder to shoulder. They looked like Mexicans, but they weren't. Fenner thought they were Spicks, but then he wasn't sure. Each of them had his right hand in the coat pocket of his tight-fiting suit. They were dressed alike: all in black, black fedoras, white shirts and dazzling ties. They looked like some turn that comes first on a vaudeville bill, only when you got a look at their eyes you began to think of snakes and things that haven't any legs.

Fenner said, 'Want to see me?' He knew without being told that two guns were pointing at his belly. The bulge in the coat pockets couldn't lie.

The shorter of the two said, 'Yeah, we thought we'd drop in.'

Fenner moved back into the office. Paula slid open the desk drawer and put her hand on Fenner's .38. The short guy said, 'Hold it.' He talked through his teeth, and he made his message convincing.

Paula sat back and folded her hands in her lap.

The short man walked into the outer office and looked round. There was a puzzled expression on his face. He went over to the big cupboard where Paula kept the stationery and looked inside. Then he grunted.

Fenner said, 'If you'll care to wait, we can give you a hot meal and a bed. We like you guys to feel at home.'

The short man picked up the heavy ash-tray that was by his hand and looked at it thoughtfully, then he smacked Fenner across his face with it very hard. Fenner dropped his head on his chest, but he didn't move quickly enough. The embossed edges of the tray caught him high up on the side of his face.

The other man pulled out a blunt-nosed automatic from his pocket and jammed it into Paula's side. He jammed it so hard that she cried out.

The short man said, 'Start something and we'll spread the twist's guts on the mat.'

Fenner pulled out his handkerchief from his breast pocket and held it to his face. The blood ran down his hand as he did so, and stained his shirt cuff. 'Maybe we'll meet again,' he said through his teeth.

'Back up against the wall. I want to look this place over,' the short man said. 'Get goin' before I hang another one on you.'

Fenner suddenly recognized them as Cubans. They were the kind you ran into on the waterfront of any coast town if you went far enough south. He stood with his back to the wall, his hands raised to his shoulders. He was so furious that he'd've taken his chance and started something if Paula hadn't been there. He somehow felt that these two were just a shade too tough to take chances.

The short Cuban ran his hands over Fenner. 'Take your coat off and give it to me,' he said.

Fenner tossed it at him. The Cuban sat on the edge of the desk and felt through the lining very carefully. He took out Fenner's note-case and examined that. Then he dropped the coat to the floor. Again he went up to Fenner and patted him all over. Fenner could smell the spiced food he had been eating recently. His fingers itched to grab him round the neck.

The Cuban stepped back and grunted. He then turned his head. 'You – come here.'

Paula's mouth set in a line, but she stood up and took a step forward. 'Don't put your filthy hands on me,' she said quietly.

The Cuban said something to the other man in Spanish. The other man jerked his head at Fenner. 'You come here.'

Fenner moved across the room, and, as he went past, the short Cuban hit him on the back of his head with his gun butt. Fenner went down on his knees, dizzily, and fell forward on his hands.

Paula opened her mouth to scream, but the other Cuban poked her with his gun barrel low down. Instead of screaming, she caught her breath in agony and folded up at the knees.

The Cuban caught her under the armpits and held her straight. The short man searched her. He didn't find what he was looking for. The other Cuban tossed her on the lounge and then sat on the corner of the table.

The short Cuban searched the office quickly. He didn't make any mess, and he acted as if he'd done that sort of job many times before. Then he went into the outer office and searched that, too.

Fenner heard him moving about, but he couldn't get his

muscles working. He tried to get up, but nothing moved at his frantic efforts. A red mist of rage and pain hung like a curtain before his eyes.

It was only when they had gone, slamming the office door behind them, that he managed to drag himself up from the floor. He put his hand on the desk to support himself, and looked round the office wildly.

Paula was sitting in a huddle on the lounge. She was crying with rage. 'Don't look at me, damn you!' she said. 'Don't look at me!'

Fenner lurched into the outer office and into the small washroom on the left. He ran the cold water into the hand basin and bathed his face carefully. The water was very red when he had finished. He walked a little more steadily to the wall cupboard and found a halfbottle of Scotch and two glasses. He took a long drink. His head ached like hell. The Scotch burnt him, but it knitted him together. He poured another two ounces into the other glass and wandered back into the office.

Paula had got herself straightened out. She was still crying quietly.

Fenner put the Scotch on the edge of the desk, near her. 'Put it down, baby,' he said. 'It's what you want.'

She looked at him and then at the Scotch. Then she reached forward and snatched up the glass. Her eyes blazed in her white face. She threw the whisky in his face.

Fenner stood very still, then he took out his bloodstained handkerchief and wiped his face. Paula put her face in her hands and began to cry properly. Fenner sat down behind his desk. He unpeeled his whisky-soaked collar and dropped it into the trash basket, then he wiped his neck carefully with the handkerchief.

They sat there for several minutes, the silence only broken by the harsh sound of Paula's sobs. Fenner felt like hell. The back of his head threatened to split open. The side of his face ached with a deadly throb, and the grazed, livid bruise on his neck smarted from the whisky. He selected a cigarette from his case with fingers that trembled a little.

Paula stopped crying. 'So you think you're tough,' she said, without taking her head from her hands. 'You think you're good, do you? You let two cheap gunmen walk in here and do this to us? My God, Dave! You're slipping. You've got soft and you've got yellow. I teamed up with you because I thought you could look after yourself and you could look after me, but I was wrong.

You sat around and got soft ... do you hear? You're yellow and you're soft! Then what do you do? You let them walk out of here and you crawl round to the bottle. Okay, Dave Fenner, I'm through.'

She beat the cushions with her clenched fists and began sobbing again. Then she said:

'Oh, Dave ... Dave ... how could you let them do that to me?'

While she had been talking Fenner just sat there, his face wooden. His eyes were half shut, and they looked like chips of ice. He said, when she had finished. 'You're right, honey. I've been sittin' around too long.' He got to his feet. 'Don't run out on me now. Just take things easy for a day or so. Shut up the office. I'm goin' to be busy.' He jerked open his desk drawer, snatched up the .38, shoved it down the front of his trouser band and adjusted the points of his vest to cover the butt. Then he walked quickly out of the office, shutting the door behind him.

An hour later, changed and neat again, Fenner thumbed a cab and gave a down-town address. As he was rushed through the heavy evening traffic he sat staring woodenly before him. Only his tightly clenched fists, that lay on each knee, indicated his suppressed feelings.

The cab swerved off Seventh Avenue and plunged into a noisy back street. A moment later it stopped, and Fenner climbed out. He tossed a dollar to the driver and picked his way across the pavement, avoiding the group of fighting kids milling around his feet.

He ran up a long flight of worn steps and rang the bell. The door opened after a while, and an old, disreputable woman squinted at him.

'Ike in?' he said shortly.

'Who wants him?'

'Tell him Fenner.'

The old woman slid the chain on the door and pulled it open. 'Careful how you go up, mister,' she said. 'Ike's restless tonight.'

Fenner pushed past her and mounted the dark stairs.

The stench of stale cooking and dirt made him wrinkle his nose. On the first landing he rapped at a door. He heard a murmur of voices, and then a sudden hush. The door opened slowly and a slim, muscular lad with a pointed chin like a hog's looked him over.

'Yeah?' he said.

'Tell Ike I want him. Fenner's the name.'

The lad shut the door. Fenner heard him say something, then he pulled the door back and jerked his head. 'Come on in,' he said.

Ike Bush was sitting at a table with four men; they were playing poker.

Fenner wandered in and stood just behind Bush. The other men looked at him suspiciously, but went on playing. Bush studied his cards thoughtfully. He was a big, fat man with a red rubbery face and ingrowing eyebrows. His thick fingers made the playing cards look like a set of dominoes.

Fenner watched him play for a few minutes. Then he leaned over and whispered in Bush's ear: 'You're goin' to take an awful hidin'.'

Bush studied the cards again, cleared his throat, and spat on the floor. He threw down the cards in disgust. Pushing back his chair, he climbed to his feet and led Fenner to the other end of the room. 'What you want?' he growled.

'Two Cubans,' Fenner said quietly. 'Both dressed in black. Black slouch hats, white shirts and flashy ties. Black square shoes. Both little punks. Both wear rods.'

Ike shook his head. 'Don't know 'em,' he said; 'they don't belong here.'

Fenner regarded him coldly. 'Then find out quick who they are. I want to get after those two fast.'

Ike shrugged. 'What've they done to you?' he said. 'I wantta get back to my game –'

Fenner turned his head slightly and showed the gash on his cheek-bone. 'Those two punks came into my joint, gave me this . . . and got away.'

Ike's eyes bulged. 'Wait,' he said. He went over to the telephone that stood on a small table across the room. After a long whispered conversation he hung up and jerked his head at Fenner.

Fenner went over to him. 'Find them?'

'Yeah.' Ike rubbed his sweaty face with the back of his hand. 'They've been in town five days. No one knows who the hell they are. They've got a joint out Brooklyn way. I got the address here. Seems they've taken a furnished house. Got dough, an' no one knows what their racket is.'

Fenner reached out and took the paper on which Ike had written the address. He got to his feet.

Ike looked at him. 'You goin' into action?' he asked curiously. 'Want one or two of the boys?'

Fenner showed his teeth in a mirthless smile. 'I can manage.' he said shortly.

Ike reached out and picked up a dark bottle without any label. He looked inquiringly at Fenner. 'One before you go?' he said.

Fenner shook his head. He patted Ike on his shoulder and walked out. The cab was still waiting. The driver leaned out as Fenner ran down the steps. 'Didn't think that was your home,' he said with a grin, 'so I hung around. Where to?'

Fenner pulled open the door. 'You might get far,' he said. 'You been learnin' your job by mail?'

The driver said seriously: 'Things are pretty bum these days. You gotta use your nut. Where to, mister?'

'The other side of Brooklyn Bridge. I'll walk the rest.'

The cab shot away from the kerb and headed for the lights of Seventh Avenue.

'Someone been knockin' you around?' the cab-driver asked curiously.

'Naw!' Fenner grunted. 'My Aunt Fanny likes to keep an edge on her teeth.'

'A tough old lady, huh?' the driver said, but after that he piped down.

It was almost dark by the time they crossed Brooklyn Bridge. Fenner paid the cab off and went into the nearest bar. He ordered a club sandwich and three fingers of rye. While he bolted the sandwich he got the girl who waited on him to find out where the address was. She took a lot of trouble, finding it on a map for him. He paid his bill, had another short rye, and went out again.

Ten minutes quick walking got him there. He found his way without asking and without making a mistake. He walked down the street, looking closely at every shadow. The house he wanted was on the corner. It was a small two-storey affair, with a square box hedge so arranged that it masked the front door completely. There were no lights showing in any of the windows. Fenner pushed open the gate and walked up the slightly inclining path. His eyes searched the black windows for any sign of movement. He didn't stop at the front door, but went on round the back of the house. There were no lights there. He found a window that was open a few inches at the top, and he shone his small torch into the room. It was empty of everything. He could see the dust on the floor-boards. It took him a few seconds to raise the window and step into the room. He was careful not to make any noise, and he trod on the boards tenderly.

Quietly he tried the door, pulled it open and stepped into a small hall. The light of his torch picked out a carpet and a large hall cupboard. The stairs faced him. He stood listening, but no sound came to him except the faint hum of distant street traffic.

He went up the stairs, the .38 in his hand. His mouth was drawn down a little at the corners, and the muscles of his face were tense. On the landing he paused again, listening. He was conscious of a strange unpleasant smell that was vaguely familiar to him. He wrinkled his nose, wondering what it could be.

There were three doors facing him. He chose the centre one. He turned the handle softly and edged the door open. The smell came to him stronger now. It reminded him of the smell from a butcher's shop. When he got the door half open, he paused and listened, then he stepped in and pushed the door to behind him. His torch lit up the light switch and he snapped it on.

He looked round the well-furnished bedroom, his finger itching on his gun trigger. There was no one there. He turned and twisted the key in the lock. He wasn't taking chances. Then he wandered round the room thoughtfully.

A woman's room. The dressing-table had the usual stuff. The bed was small, and a big nightdress case in the shape of a flaxen-haired doll lay on the pillow.

Fenner went over to the wardrobe and looked inside. There was one costume hanging on the peg. Nothing more. There didn't have to be anything more; it was the costume that Marian Daley had worn when she called on him.

Fenner touched it thoughtfully while he tried to visualize Marian Daley. He took the costume out of the cupboard and tossed it on the bed. There was more spring in his step as he went over to the chest of drawers. In the top drawer was the prim little hat. He tossed that on the bed too. In another drawer he found a bundle of underclothes, a suspender girdle, stockings and shoes. He threw all these on to the bed. Then he went over to the dressing-table and jerked open the small drawer under the mirror. Stuffed inside was her handbag. He pulled it out with difficulty, and walked with it across the room. He sat on the bed, slapping the bag on his open palm and staring hard at the carpet. He didn't like this at all.

He opened the bag and spilled the contents on to the bed. The usual junk a woman carries around clattered into a small, rather pathetic pile. He stirred the pile with his finger and then looked in the bag again. There was nothing there that he could see, and he put two fingers inside and ripped out the lining. Crumpled at the bottom of the bag, either hidden there, or else slipped through the lining, was a piece of paper. He spread it out and peered at it. It was a letter on a single sheet of notepaper in a large careless hand. It read:

Key West.

Dear Marian,
Don't worry. Noolen has promised to help me. Pio doesn't know anything yet. I think things will come out all right now

The letter was unsigned.

Fenner folded the paper carefully and put it in his cigarette-case. He sat on the bed, thinking. Key West and the two Cubans. Something was beginning to add up. He got to his feet and made a systematic search of the whole room, but he found nothing else. Then he unlocked the door, snapped off the light and stepped quietly into the passage.

He eased his way into the room on the left. His torch showed him that it was a fair-sized bathroom. Making sure that the curtain was drawn over the window he reached out for the light switch. The smell in the room was making him feel a little sick. He knew now what it was and he was steeling himself to turn on the light. It flashed on as he turned the switch down with exaggerated care.

In the hard light the room looked like an abattoir after a full day's work. The bath stood against the wall and was covered with a blood-spotted sheet. The wall was marked red and the floor by the bath was red. A table stood near the bath and that, too, had a blood-soaked towel on it. Fenner could see that it covered something.

He stood very still, looking round the room, his face white and set. He took a slow step forward and, hooking his gun-barrel under the towel, he flicked it off the table. A slender white arm rolled off the table and fell on the floor at his feet.

Fenner felt the cold sweat of sickness break out all over him.

He hastily swallowed the sudden rush of saliva that filled his mouth. He looked at the arm carefully, but he couldn't bring himself to touch it. The hand was narrow and long, with carefully manicured finger-nails. There was no doubt about it. The arm and hand belonged to a woman.

With a hand that shook a little, he lit a cigarette, drawing the smoke down into his lungs and forcing it through his nostrils, trying to get rid of the nauseating smell of death. Then he walked over to the bath and turned back the sheet.

Fenner was tough. He'd been in the newspaper racket for years, and sudden death didn't mean much to him. Violence was just another headline, but this business shook him. It shook him more because he'd known her. She was his client, and only a few hours before she had been a living woman.

The thing in the bath told him he couldn't be wrong. The tell-tale vivid bruises still decorated her body.

Fenner dropped the sheet and stepped out of the room. He pulled the door gently to and leaned against it. He'd have given a lot for a drink. He stood there, his mind blank, until the first shock drifted away from him. Then he wiped his face with his handkerchief and moved to the head of the stairs.

Grosset had to hear about this. He'd got to get those two Cubans fast. He stood thinking. That was it. They were planting her somewhere and they'd be back to get rid of the body.

Fenner's eyes narrowed. All he had to do now was to wait for them to come back, and then give it to them. Before he could make up his mind whether to hunt for a 'phone and get in touch with Grosset or to just wait and handle it on his own, he heard a car draw up outside and a car door slam.

He stepped quietly back into the bedroom, letting the .38 slide into his hand. He stood inside the room, holding the door open a few inches.

He heard the front door open and shut. Then a light snapped on in the hall. He moved out a little and peered over the banisters. The two Cubans were standing in the hall. They were very tense, listening. Fenner remained where he was, motionless. He saw them exchange glances. Then the short one murmured something to the other, who put his case down and came up the stairs fast. He came up so fast Fenner hadn't time to duck back.

The Cuban saw him as he rounded the bend in the stairway and his hand flew to the inside of his coat. Fenner drew his lips off his teeth and shot him three times. The noise of the gun crashed through the still house. The Cuban caught his breath in a sob and bent forward, holding himself low down.

Fenner jumped forward, heaved him out of the way, and dived down the stairway as if he were taking a header into the water.

The short Cuban had no chance to get out of the way. The sudden crash of gunfire had paralysed him, and although his hand went unconsciously to his hip, he could not move his feet.

Fenner's fourteen stone of bone and muscle hit him like a shell. They both crashed down on to the floor, the Cuban underneath. The Cuban had given one high-pitched squeal of terror as he saw something coming at him, then Fenner was on him.

The crash made Fenner's head spin and for a second or two he was so dazed that he could only lie, crushing the Cuban flat. His gun had shot out of his hand as he went down, and as he struggled to his knees he was dimly conscious of a jabbing pain in his arms.

The Cuban didn't move. Fenner cautiously got to his feet and stirred him with his foot. The odd angle of the Cuban's head told him all he wanted to know. He'd broken his neck.

He went on his knee and searched the Cuban's pockets, but he didn't find anything. He looked inside one of the suit-cases, but it was empty. The smear of blood on the lining confirmed his idea that they were taking the body away in bits.

He found his gun and cautiously went upstairs to have a look at the other Cuban. He, too, was as dead as a pork chop. He lay twisted in a corner, his mouth drawn up, showing his teeth. Fenner thought he looked like a mad dog. A quick search revealed nothing, and Fenner went downstairs again. He wanted to get out of this fast. He turned off the light in the hall, opened the front door and stepped out into the night.

Ouside, the car still waited. There was no one in it, but Fenner let it stay. He walked down the street, keeping in the shadow, and it was only when he got into the Fulton Street crowds that he relaxed at all.

A taxi took him back to his office. During the short ride he had decided on a plan of action. He took the elevator up to the fourth floor and hurried down the passage to his office.

A light was still burning, and for a moment he hesitated before entering. Then, keeping his hand on his gun, he turned the handle and walked in.

Paula was sitting in an arm-chair before the telephone. She jerked up her head quickly as if she'd been asleep.

'Why haven't you gone home?' Fenner said shortly.

Paula indicated the telephone. 'She might have rung,' she said quietly.

Fenner sat down beside her wearily.

Paula said, 'Dave, I'm sorry about —'

'Skip it,' Dave said, patting her hand. 'You were right to blow off. Right now things are happenin'. Those two Cubans got hold of that girl and killed her. I caught them cartin' her away. They're dead. I killed 'em both. Don't interrupt. Let me tell you fast. The cops must be kept out of this. This is between me and whoever started it. Those cheap punks are only the dressin'. They ain't the whole salad. Take a look at that.' He gave Paula the letter he'd found in Marian's bag.

Paula read it through. Her face had gone a little pale, but otherwise she was calm. 'Key West?' she said.

Fenner's smile was mirthless. 'That make you think?'

Paula puzzled.

'That dame wanted to find her sister. She said she didn't know where she was. Why didn't she tell me Key West? You know, baby, it looks like a plant. There's something very funny about this business.'

'Who's Pio?' Paula said, reading the letter again. 'And who's Noolen?'

Fenner shook his head. There was a hard look in his eyes. 'I don't know, baby, but I'm goin' to find out. I've got six thousand dollars of that girl's money, an' if I have to spend every dollar of it, I'm goin' to find out.'

He went over to the telephone and dialled a number. While the line was connecting, he said, 'Ike's goin' to earn some of that dough I've been slippin' him.'

The line connected with a little plop. Fenner said, 'Ike?' He waited, then he said, 'Tell him Fenner. Tell him if he don't come to this 'phone at once, I'll come down and kick his teeth in.' He waited again, his right shoe kicking the desk leg continuously. Then Ike's growl came over the wire.

'All right, all right,' Fenner said. 'To hell with your game. This is urgent. I want to find someone I can contact in Key West. Do you know anyone down there? He's gotta have an in with the guys that count.'

'Key West?' Ike grumbled. 'I don't know anyone in Key West.'

Fenner showed his teeth. 'Then hustle up someone who does. Ring me back right away. I'll wait.' He slammed the receiver down on its cradle.

Paula said, 'You going down there?'

Fenner nodded. 'It's a long way, but I think that's where it'll finish. Maybe I'm wrong, but I'm going to see.'

Paula got to her feet. 'Do I go with you?'

'You stick around here, baby. If I think something's goin' to start, I'll have you down. Right now you'll be more of a help here. Grosset's got to be looked after. Tell him I'm out of town for a few days, but you don't know where.'

'I'll go over to your place and pack a bag for you.'

Fenner nodded. 'Yeah,' he said, 'do that.'

When she had gone, he went over to his reference shelf and checked the Pan-American air time-table. There was a 'plane for Florida at 12.30. He glanced at his watch. It was five past eleven. If Ike 'phoned back quickly, he could just make it.

He sat behind his desk and lit a cigarette. He had to wait twenty minutes before the 'phone jangled. He snatched the receiver.

'The guy you want is Buck Nightingale,' Ike said. 'He's got his finger in most pies down there. Treat him easy, he's gotta brittle temper.'

'So have I,' Fenner said unpleasantly. 'Fix it for me, Ike. Tell him that Dave Ross'll be down on the next 'plane an' wants introductions. Give me a good build up. I'll tell Paula to put a cheque in the mail for five hundred bucks for your trouble.'

'Sure, sure.' Ike's voice was quite oily. 'I'll fix it for you,' and he hung up.

Fenner dialled another number. 'Paula?' he said. 'Hurry with that packing. I'm catching the 12.30 'plane. Meet me at the airport as fast as you can make it.'

He pulled open a drawer, took out a cheque-book and signed five blank cheques quickly. He put his hat and coat on and looked round the office thoughtfully. Then he snapped off the electric light and went out, slamming the door behind him.

Chapter Two

Fenner arrived at Key West about nine. He checked in at a nearby hotel, had a cold bath and went to bed. He was lulled to sleep by the drone of an electric fan that buzzed just above his head.

He had two hours' catnap, then the telephone woke him. The telephone said 'Good morning.' He ordered orange juice and toast and told the voice at the other end to send him up a bottle of Scotch. While he was waiting, he went into the bathroom and had a cold shower.

It was half-past eleven when he left the hotel. He walked south down Roosevelt Boulevard. All the time he walked he kept thinking about the heat. He thought if he was going to stay long in this burg he'd certainly have to do something about the heat.

He stopped a policeman and asked for Buck Nightingale's place.

The cop gaped at him. 'You're new here, huh?'

Fenner said, 'No, I'm the oldest inhabitant. That's why I come up an' ask you. I wantta see if you know the answer,' and he went on, telling himself that he'd have to be careful. Already the heat was doing things to his temper.

He found Nightingale's place by asking a taxi-driver. He got the information and he got civility. He thanked the driver, then spoiled it by not hiring the cab. The driver told him he'd take him all over the town for twenty-five cents. Fenner said that he'd rather walk. He went on, closing his ears to what the driver said. It was too hot to fight, anyway.

By the time he reached Flagler Avenue his feet began to hurt. It was like walking on a red-hot stove. At the corner of Flagler and Thompson he gave up and flagged a cab. When he settled himself in the cab he took off his shoes and gave his feet some air. He'd no sooner got his shoes off than the cab forced itself against the oncoming traffic and pulled up outside a small shop.

The driver twisted his head. 'This is it, boss,' he said.

Fenner squeezed his feet into his shoes and had difficulty in getting his hot hand into his trouser pocket. He gave the driver twenty-five cents and got out of the cab. The shop was very clean and the windows shone. In the right-hand window stood a small white coffin. The back of the window was draped with heavy black curtains. Fenner, fascinated, thought the coffin looked lonely all by itself. He read the card that stood on a small easel by the coffin.

> MAY WE LOOK AFTER YOUR LITTLE ONE
> IF THE LORD DOES NOT SPARE HIM

Fenner thought it was all in very good taste. He went over to the other window and inspected that, too. Again, it was draped in black curtains, and on a white pedestal stood a silver urn. A card bearing the simple inscription "Dust to Dust" impressed him.

He stepped back and read the facia over the shop:

B. NIGHTINGALE'S FUNERAL PARLOUR.

'Well, well,' he said, 'quite a joint.'

He walked into the shop. As he opened the door the electric buzzer started, and stopped as soon as the door shut. Inside, the shop was even more impressive. There was a short counter dividing the room exactly in half. This was draped with a white-and-purple velvet cover. Several black leather arm-chairs dotted the purple pile carpet. On the left of the room was a large glass cabinet containing miniature coffins made of every conceivable material, from gold to pine wood.

On the right was a six-foot crucifix cleverly illuminated by concealed lights. The figure was so realistic that it quite startled Fenner. He felt that he'd wandered into a church.

Long white, black and purple drapes hung behind the counter. There was no one in the shop. Fenner wandered over to the cabinet and examined the coffins. He thought that as a permanent home the gold one was a swell job.

A woman came quietly from behind the curtain. She wore a tight-fitting black silk dress, white collar and cuffs. She was a blonde, and her big gash-like mouth was very red with paint. She looked at Fenner and her mouth shaped into a smile. Fenner thought she was quite something.

She said in a low, solemn voice, 'Can I help you, please?'

Fenner scratched his chin. 'Do you sell these boxes?' he said, jerking his thumb in the direction of the glass case.

She blinked. 'Why, sure,' she said. 'They're just models, you know; but was that what you wanted?'

Fenner shook his head. 'No,' he said; 'I was just curious.'

She looked at him doubtfully.

Fenner went on: 'Nightingale in?'

'Did you want to see him particularly?'

'That's why I asked, baby. Tell him Ross.'

She said, 'I'll see. He's very busy right now.'

Fenner watched her go away behind the curtain. He thought her shape from behind was pretty good.

She came back after a while and said, 'Will you come up?'

He followed her behind the curtain and up the short flight of stairs. He liked the scent she used, and halfway up the stairs he told her so. She looked over her shoulder at him and smiled. She had big white teeth. 'What do I do now?' she said. 'Should my face go red?'

He shook his head seriously. 'I just like to tell a dame when she's good,' he said.

She pointed to a door. 'He's in there,' she said. Then, after a little pause, she said, 'I like you. You've got nice eyes,' and she went downstairs, patting her blonde curls with long white fingers.

Fenner fingered his tie. 'Some frill,' he thought, and turned the door handle and walked in.

The room was obviously a workshop. Four coffins stood in a line on trestles. Nightingale was screwing a brass plate on one of them.

Nightingale was a little dark man with thick-lensed steel-rimmed glasses. His skin was very white, and two large colourless eyes blinked weakly at Fenner from behind the cheaters.

Fenner said, 'I'm Ross.'

Nightingale went on screwing down the plate. 'Yes?' he said. 'Did you want to see me?'

'Dave Ross,' Fenner repeated, standing by the door. 'I think you were expectin' me.'

Nightingale put down the screwdriver and looked at him. 'So I was,' he said, as if remembering. 'So I was. We'll go upstairs and talk.'

Fenner followed him out of the workshop and up another short flight of stairs. Nightingale showed him into a room which was large and cool. Two big windows opened out to a small balcony. From the window Fenner could see the Mexican Gulf.

Nightingale said, 'Sit down. Take off your coat if you want to.'

Fenner took off his coat and rolled up his sleeves. He sat by the window.

Nightingale said, 'Perhaps a drink?'

'Sure.'

When the drinks were fixed, and Nightingale had settled himself, Fenner sparred for an opening. He knew he'd have to go carefully with this little guy. He didn't know how far he could trust him. It was no use getting him suspicious.

He said at last, 'How far you carryin' me?'

Nightingale fingered his glass with his thick weak fingers. He looked a little bewildered. 'All the way,' he said. 'That's what you want, isn't it?'

Fenner stretched out. 'I want to get in with the boys. New York's got too hot for me.'

'I can do that,' Nightingale said simply. 'Crotti said you were an all-right guy and I was to help you. Crotti's been good to me; I'm glad to even things up with him.'

Fenner guessed Crotti was the guy Ike got on to.

'Maybe five C's would be more concrete than lovin' Crotti,' he said drily.

Nightingale looked a little hurt. 'I don't want your dough,' he said simply. 'Crotti said "help this man," and that's enough for me.'

Fenner twisted in his chair. It quite shocked him to see that the little man was sincere.

'Swell,' he said hastily. 'Don't get me wrong. Where I come from there's a different set of morals.'

'I can give you introductions. But what is it exactly that you want?'

Fenner wished he knew. He stalled. 'I guess I gotta get into the money again,' he said. 'Maybe one of your crowd could use me.'

'Crotti says you've got quite a reputation. He says you've got notches on your gun.'

Fenner tried to look modest and cursed Ike's imagination. 'I get along,' he said casually.

'Maybe Carlos could use you.'

Fenner tried a venture. 'I thought Noolen might be good to throw in with.'

Nightingale's watery eyes suddenly flashed. 'Noolen? Noolen's the south end of a horse.'

'So?'

'Carlos has Noolen with his pants down. You won't get any place with a piker like Noolen.'

Fenner gathered that Noolen was a wash-out. He tried again.

'You surprise me. I was told Noolen was quite a big shot around here.'

Nightingale stretched his neck and deliberately spat on the floor. 'Nuts,' he said.

'Who's Carlos?'

Nightingale got back his good humour. 'He's the boy. Now, Pío'll get you somewhere.'

Fenner slopped a little of his Scotch. 'That his name – Pío Carlos?'

Nightingale nodded. 'He's got this burg like that.' He held out his small squat hand and closed his thick fingers into a small fist. 'Like that – see?'

Fenner nodded. 'Okay,' he said, 'I'll be guided by you.'

Nightingale got up and put his glass on the table. 'I've got a little job to do, and then we'll go down and meet the boys. You rest here. It's too hot to go runnin' around.'

When he had gone, Fenner shut his eyes and thought. The lid was coming off this quicker than he'd imagined. He'd have to watch his step.

He felt a little draught and he opened his eyes. The blonde had come in and was gently shutting the door. Fenner heard her turn the key in the lock. 'Jumpin' snakes,' he thought, 'she's goin' to grab me!'

He swung his legs off the chair Nightingale had sat in, and struggled to his feet.

'Stay put,' she said, coming over. 'I want to talk to you.'

Fenner sat down again. 'What's your name, honey?' he said, stalling for time.

'Robbins,' she said. 'They call me Curly round here.'

'Nice name, Curly,' Fenner said. 'What's on your mind?'

She sat down in Nightingale's chair. 'Take my tip,' she said, keeping her voice low, 'an' go home. Imported tough guys don't stand up long in this town.'

Fenner raised his eyebrows. 'Who told you I was a tough guy?' he said.

'I don't have to be told. You've come down here to set fire to the place, haven't you? Well, it won't work. These hoods here don't like foreign competition. You'll be cat's meat in a few days if you stick around.'

Fenner was quite touched. 'You're bein' a very nice little girl,' he said; 'but I'm afraid it's no soap. I'm down here for a livin', and I'm stickin'.'

She sighed. 'I thought you'd take it like that,' she said, getting up. 'If you knew what's good for you, you'd take a powder quick. Anyway, watch out. I don't trust any of them. Don't trust Nightingale. He looks a punk, but he isn't. He's a killer, so watch him.'

Fenner climbed out of his chair. 'Okay, baby,' he said. 'I'll watch him. Now you'd better blow, before he finds you here.' He led her to the door.

She said, 'I'm tellin' you this because you're cute. I hate seein' a big guy like you headin' for trouble.'

Fenner grinned, and, swinging his hand, he gave her a gentle smack. 'Don't you worry your brains about me,' he said.

She leaned towards him, raising her face; so, because he thought she was pretty good, he kissed her. She wound her arms round his neck and held him. They stood like that for several minutes, then Fenner pushed her away gently.

She stood looking at him, breathing hard. 'I guess I'm crazy,' she said, colour suddenly flooding her face.

Fenner ran his finger round the inside of his collar. 'I'm a bit of a bug myself,' he said. 'Scram, baby, before we really get to work. Beat it, an' I'll see you in church.'

She went out quickly and shut the door. Fenner took out his handkerchief and wiped his hands thoughtfully. 'I think I'm goin' to like this job,' he said aloud. 'Yeah, it might develop into somethin',' and he went back and sat down by the open window again.

Nightingale led him through the crowded lobby of the Flagler Hotel. Fenner said, 'This guy does himself well.'

Nightingale stopped before the elevator doors and thumbed the automatic button. 'Sure,' he said; 'what did I tell you? Pío's the boy to be in with.'

Fenner studied the elaborate wrought ironwork of the gates. 'You're tellin' me,' he said.

The cage came to rest and they stepped in. Nightingale pressed the button for the fifth, and the cage shot them up.

'Now I'll do the talkin',' Nightingale said, as the lift stopped. 'Maybe you won't get anythin', but I'll try.'

Fenner grunted and followed the little man down the corridor. He stopped outside No. 47 and rapped three times fast and twice slowly, on the door.

'Secret signs as well,' Fenner said admiringly.

The door opened and a short Cuban, dressed in a black suit,

looked them over. Fenner shaped his lips for a whistle, but he didn't make any sound.

Nightingale said in his soft voice: 'It's all right.'

The Cuban let them in. As he shut the door after them, Fenner saw a bulge in his hip-pocket. The hall they found themselves in was big, and three doors faced them.

'The boys in yet?' Nightingale asked.

The Cuban nodded. He sat down in an arm-chair by the front door and picked up a newspaper again. As far as he was concerned they weren't there.

Nightingale went into the centre room. There were four men lounging about the room. They were all in shirt-sleeves and they all were smoking. Two of them were reading newspapers, one of them was listening to the radio, and the fourth was cleaning a rod. They all glanced at Nightingale, and then fixed wooden looks on Fenner.

The man with the rod got up slowly. 'Who is it?' he said. He'd got a way of speaking with his teeth shut. He wore a white suit and a black shirt with a white tie. His wiry black hair was cropped close, and his yellow-green eyes were cold and suspicious.

Nightingale said, 'This is Ross. From New York. Crotti knows him. He's all right.' Then he turned to Fenner. 'Meet Reiger.'

Fenner gave Reiger a wintry smile. He didn't like the look of him.

Reiger nodded. 'How do,' he said. 'Stay'n' long?'

Fenner waved his hand. 'These other guys friends of yours, or are they just decoration?'

Reiger's eyes snapped. 'I said, stayin' long?' he said.

Fenner eyed him. 'I heard you. It ain't no goddam business of yours, is it?'

Nightingale put his hand on Fenner's cuff. He didn't say anything, but it was a little warning gesture. Reiger tried a staring match with Fenner, lost it and shrugged. He said, 'Pug Kane by the radio. Borg on the right. Miller on the left.'

The three other men nodded at Fenner. None of them seemed friendly.

Fenner was quite at ease. 'Glad to know you,' he said. 'I won't ask you guys for a drink. Maybe you don't use the stuff.'

Reiger turned on Nightingale. 'What's this?' he snarled. 'Who's this loud-mouthed punk?'

Miller, a fat, greasy-looking man with a prematurely bald head said, 'Somethin' he's dug outa an ash-can.'

Fenner walked over to him very quickly and slapped him twice across his mouth. A gun jumped into Nightingale's hand and he said, 'Don't start anythin' – don't start anythin', please.'

Fenner was surprised they took any notice of Nightingale, but they did. They all froze solid. Even Reiger looked a little sick.

Nightingale said to Fenner, 'Come away from him.' His voice had enough menace in it to chill Fenner a trifle. Curly was right. This guy was a killer.

Fenner stepped away from Miller and put his hands in his pockets.

Nightingale said, 'I won't have it. When I bring a friend of mine up here, you treat him right. I'd like to measure some of you heels for a box.'

Fenner laughed. 'Ain't that against etiquette?' he said. 'Or do you take it both ways? Bump 'em an' bury 'em?'

Nightingale put his rod away, and the others relaxed. Reiger said with a little forced smile, 'This heat plays hell.' He went over to a cupboard and set up drinks.

Fenner sat down close to Reiger. He thought this one was the meanest of the bunch and he was the one to work on. He said quietly, 'This heat even makes me hate myself.'

Reiger looked at him still suspiciously. 'Forget it,' he said. 'Now you're here, make yourself at home.'

Fenner rested his nose on the rim of his glass. 'Carlos in?' he said.

Reiger's eyes opened. 'Carlos ain't got time for visitors,' he said. 'I'll tell him you've been in.'

Fenner drained his glass and stood up. Nightingale made a move, but Fenner stopped him with a gesture. He stood looking round at each man in turn. He said, 'Well, I'm glad I looked in. I thought this was a live outfit, an' I find I'm wrong. You guys are no use to me. You think you've got this town by the shorts, but you're fat an' lazy. You think you're the big-shots, but that's where you're wrong. I think I'll go an' see Noolen. That guy's supposed to be the south end of a horse. All right, then I'll make him the north end. It'll be more amusing than playin' around with guys like you.'

Reiger slid his hand inside his coat, but Nightingale already had his rod out. 'Hold it,' he said.

The four men sat still; their angry faces made Fenner want to laugh.

Nightingale said, 'I asked him to come along. If he don't like us, then let him go. A friend of Crotti's's a friend of mine.'

Fenner said, 'I'll drop round some time an' see you again.'

He walked out of the room, past the Cuban, who ignored him, and took the elevator down to the street level.

The commissionaire at the door looked as if he had some brains. Fenner asked him if he knew where he could find Noolen. The commissionaire said he'd got an office off Duval Street, and beckoned a cab. Fenner gave him a fin.

The commissionaire helped him into the cab as though he were made of china.

Noolen's office was over a shop. Fenner had to go up a long flight of stairs before he located the frosted gass-panelled door. When he got inside, a flat-chested woman whose thirties were crowding up on her, regarded him suspiciously from behind a typewriter.

'Noolen in?' he asked, smiling at her, because he felt she could do with a few male smiles.

'He's busy right now,' she said. 'Who is it?'

'Me? Tell him Ross. Dave Ross. Tell him I ain't sellin' anythin', and I want to see him fast.'

She got up and walked over to a door behind her. Fenner gave her a start, then he took two strides and walked into the room with her.

Noolen was a dark, middle-aged man, growing a paunch. He'd a double chin and a hooked nose. His eyes were hooded and mean. He looked at Fenner and then at the woman. 'Who's this?' he snapped.

The woman jerked round, her eyes popping. 'Wait outside,' she said.

Fenner pushed past her and wandered over to the big desk. He noticed a lot of spots on Noolen's vest. He noticed the dirty nails and the grubby hands. Nightingale was right. Noolen *was* the south end of a horse.

Fenner said, 'Ross is the name. How do?'

Noolen jerked his head at the woman, who went out, shutting the door with a sharp click. 'What do you want?' he asked, scowling.

Fenner put his hands on the desk and leant forward. 'I want a hook-up in this burg. I've seen Carlos. He won't play. You're next on my list, so here I am.'

Noolen said, 'Where you from?'

'Crotti.'

Noolen studied his dirty finger-nails. 'So Carlos couldn't use you. What's the matter with him?' There was a sneer in his voice.

'Carlos didn't see me. I saw his flock of hoods an' that was enough for me. They made me puke, so I scrammed.'

'Why come to me?'

Fenner grinned. 'They told me you were the south end of a horse. I thought maybe we could do something about it.'

A faint red crept into Noolen's face. 'So they said that, did they?'

'Sure. With me, you might have a lotta fun with that gang.'

'Meanin'?'

Fenner hooked a chair towards him with his foot and sat down. He leant forward and helped himself to a thin greenish cigar from a cigar-box on the desk. He took his time lighting it. Noolen sat watching him. His eyes intent and bright.

'Look at it this way,' Fenner said, stretching in the chair; 'my way. I've come from Crotti. I want a chance like the rest of you for some easy dough an' not much excitement. Crotti said either Carlos or Noolen. Carlos's mob is too busy big-shotting to worry about me. I can't even get in to see Carlos. You – I walk in an' find you sittin' around with a flat-chested bird outside as your muscle guard. Why did Crotti tip you? Maybe you've been someone an' Crotti's getting behind in the news. Maybe you are someone, an' this is a front. Take it all round, I think you an' me might get places.'

Noolen gave a little shrug. He shook his head. 'Not just now,' he said. 'I don't know Crotti. I've never heard of him, an' I don't believe you've come from him. I think you're a punk gunman bluffing himself a job. I don't want you an' I hope I'll never want you.'

Fenner got up and yawned. 'That's swell,' he said. 'I can now grab myself a little rest. When you've looked into things, you'll find me at the Haworth Hotel. If you know Nightingale, have a word with him – he thinks I'm quite a boy.'

He nodded to Noolen and walked out of the office. He went down the stairs, called a cab, and drove to his hotel. He went into the restaurant and ordered a turtle steak. While he was eating, Nightingale came in and sat down opposite him.

Fenner said, with his mouth full, 'Ain't you got any boxes to make, or is business bad?'

Nightingale looked worried. 'That was a hell of a thing to do – walking out like that.'

'Yeah? I always walk out when I get a Bronx cheer. Why not?'

'Listen, Reiger ain't soft. That ain't the way to handle Reiger.'

'No? You tell me.'

Nightingale ordered some brown bread, cheese and a glass of milk. He kept his eyes on the white tablecloth until the waitress brought the order, and when she had gone away he said, 'This makes it difficult for me.'

Fenner put his knife and fork down. He smiled at the little man. 'I like you,' he said. 'You're the one guy who's given me a hand up to now. Suppose you stick around, I might do you some good.'

Nightingale peered at Fenner from under his hat. The sun, coming in through the slatted blinds, reflected on his glasses. 'You might do me some harm, too,' he said dryly.

Fenner resumed his eating. 'Hell!' he said. 'This is a hell of a burg, ain't it?'

When they had finished their meal, Fenner pushed his chair away and stood up. 'Okay, pal,' he said. 'I'll be seeing you.'

Nightingale said, 'We might talk some time.' He said it hopefully.

Fenner took off his hat and ran his fingers through his hair. 'I don't know,' he said vaguely, 'I don't know.'

He nodded to the little man and went out to the office. The hotel manager was busy at the desk. He looked up as Fenner passed and gave an oily smile.

Fenner said, 'I'm goin' to sleep. This place's killin' me.'

Before the manager could say anything, he went on up the stairs to his bedroom. He shut the door and turned the key. Then he took off his coat and hat and lay on the bed. He went to sleep almost immediately, a pleased smile on his mouth.

The 'phone woke him. He sat up with a jerk, glanced at the clock, saw he had slept for two hours, and reached out for the 'phone.

A voice said, 'Come over to the Flagler Hotel right away. The boss wants you.'

Fenner screwed up his eyes. 'Tell the boss I came this mornin'. I don't visit the same place twice,' and hung up.

He lay back on the bed and shut his eyes. He only lay there a minute or so before the 'phone went again.

The same voice said, 'You'd better come. Carlos don't like bein' kept waitin'.'

Fenner said, 'Tell Carlos to come out here, or tell him to go roll a hoop.' He put the receiver on the prong with exaggerated care.

He didn't bother to answer the 'phone when it rang again. He went into the little bathroom, bathed his face, gave himself a short shot from the Scotch, put on his hat and coat, and went downstairs.

The heat of the afternoon sun was blistering. The hotel lobby was deserted. He went over and sat down near the entrance. He put his hat on the floor beside him and stared out into the street. He knew that he wasn't going to get very far with this business unless he turned up Marian Daley's sister. He wondered whether the cops had found the two Cubans and the remains of Marian. He wondered what Paula was doing. From where he sat he could look into the hot, deserted street. A big touring car suddenly swept into the street, roared down to the hotel, and skidded to a standstill.

Fenner relaxed into the long cane chair and, reaching down, picked up his hat and put it on.

There were four men in the car. Three of them got out, leaving the driver sitting behind the wheel.

Fenner recognized Reiger and Miller, but the other guy he didn't know. They came up the few steps quickly and blinked round in the semi-gloom. Reiger saw Fenner almost at once. He came over.

Fenner looked up at him and nodded. 'Want to see anyone?' he said casually. 'The clerk's gone bye-bye.'

Reiger said, 'Carlos wants you. Come on.'

Fenner shook his head. 'It's too hot. Tell him some other time.'

The other two came and stood round. They looked mean. Reiger said softly, 'Comin' on your dogs, or do we carry you?'

Fenner got up slowly. 'If it's like that,' he said, and went with them to the car. He knew Reiger was itching to slug him and he knew it wouldn't do any good to make too much fuss. He wanted to see Carlos, but he wanted them to think he wasn't too interested.

They drove to the Flagler Hotel in silence. Fenner sat between Reiger and Miller, and the other man, whom they called Bugsey, sat with the driver.

They all went up in the small elevator and along to No. 47. As they entered, Fenner said, 'You could have saved yourself a trip by playin' ball this mornin'.'

Reiger didn't say anything. He crossed the room and rapped on another door and went in. Bugsey followed behind Fenner.

Carlos lay on a couch before a big open window. He was dressed in a cream silk dressing-gown, patterned with large red flowers. A white silk handkerchief was folded carefully in a stock at his throat, and his bare feet were encased in red Turkish slippers.

He was smoking a marihuana cigarette, and round his brown, hairy wrist hung a gold-linked bracelet.

Carlos was young. Maybe he was twenty or maybe he was twenty-four. His face was the colour of old parchment and he had very red lips. Thin lips, paper-thin lips, and red, just like someone had slit his throat with a razor and moved the wound above his chin. His nose was small, with very wide nostrils, and his ears lay tightly against his head. His eyes were large and fringed with dark curly eyelashes. He had no expression in them. They were like dull pieces of black glass. His hair grew away from his forehead on either side of his temples. It was black, glistening, and inclined to wave. Take a quick look at Carlos, and you'd think he was a pretty handsome guy, but when you looked again you got an eyeful of his mouth and his lobeless ears, and you weren't sure. When you got to his eyes you were dead certain that he was bad.

Reiger said, 'This is Ross,' then he went out with Bugsey.

Fenner nodded to Carlos and sat down. He sat a little way from the sickening smoke of the marihuana cigarette.

Carlos looked at him with his blank eyes. 'What is it?' he said. His voice was hoarse and unmusical.

'This mornin' I came round to see you, but your hoods told me you were busy or somethin'. I ain't used to bein' handled that way, so I went back to my dump. I ain't sure I wantta talk to you now.'

Carlos let his leg slide off the couch on to the floor. 'I'm a cautious man,' he said; 'I have to be. When I heard you'd been in, I got on long-distance to Crotti. I wanted to know more about you first – that's reasonable, I think?'

Fenner's eyelids narrowed. 'Sure,' he said.

'Crotti says you're all right.'

Fenner shrugged. 'So what?'

'I can use you. But you gotta show me you're my type of guy.'

'Let me hang around for a bit. Maybe you ain't my type of guy either.'

Carlos smiled. There was no mirth in it. 'You've got a lot of confidence. That's all right in its way.'

Fenner stood up. 'I get along,' he said abruptly. 'Where do we go from here?'

Carlos got off the couch. 'Go an' talk to the boys,' he said. 'Then we'll go down to the waterfront. I've got a little job to do. It'll interest you.'

Fenner said, 'Do I come on your pay-roll?'

'Suppose we say a hundred bucks until we get used to each other?'

'We've got to get used to each other pretty quick,' Fenner said without humour. 'That's chicken-feed to me.'

He went out and shut the door behind him.

Fenner, Carlos, Reiger and Bugsey entered a coffee-shop an hour later. The place was full, and curious eyes watched them walk to the back through a curtained door and out of sight.

Fenner found that Bugsey was ready to be friendly. He was a short, thick-set man, very much inclined to fat, with a round mottled face, gooseberry laughing eyes, and lips like sausages.

Reiger hated Fenner, and they both knew it. He walked with Carlos, and Fenner and Bugsey tagged along behind. They went down a short passage and down a flight of stairs. It was dark and rank in the passage, and very silent. At the bottom of the stairs was a door. Carlos unlocked it and went in.

The room was very large, and Fenner noticed, when Bugsey pushed the door to, he had to use a lot of beef. The door was solid and shut to with a thud.

The room was dark but for two clots of brilliant light at the far end. Carlos and Reiger went towards the light and Fenner stood still. He looked inquiringly at Bugsey.

Bugsey pursed up his mouth. 'This is his office,' he said in a low voice.

'What do we do – just stand around?'

Bugsey nodded.

Carlos sat down at a big table under one of the pools of light. He said to Reiger, 'Bring him in.'

Reiger went into the darkness, and Fenner heard him unlock a door. A minute or so later he came back dragging a man with him. He led him by the front of his coat just like he was a sack of coal, not looking at him, not seemingly aware that he was bringing him in. He went over to a chair close to Carlos and dumped the man into it.

Fenner wandered a little nearer. The man was Chinese. He wore a shabby black suit and he sat huddled in the chair, his hands under his armpits and his body bent double.

Fenner looked at Bugsey, who again pursed his lips, but this time he didn't say anything.

Reiger dragged the Chinese's head back.

Fenner made a slight movement forward, then stopped. The man's face glistened in the bright light. His skin was so tightly stretched that his face was skull-like. His lips had shrunk off his teeth, and only black shadows showed where his eyes were.

Carlos said, 'You goin' to write that letter now?'

The Chinese just sat there, silent. Reiger jerked on his pigtail, wrenching his head back and then jerking it forward.

Carlos smiled. 'An obstinate punk, ain't he, Reiger?' He pulled open a drawer and took something out, which he put on the table. 'Put his hand on the table.'

Reiger put his hand on the skinny wrist and pulled. The man kept his hands hidden under his armpits and Fenner could see the tremendous effort he made to keep them there. There was a long silence while Reiger struggled. Fenner could see the hand coming inch by inch from its sanctuary. Beads of perspiration started out on the Chinese's face and a low moaning sound came through his teeth.

Fenner said to Bugsey, 'What the hell's this?'

Bugsey waved at him, but said nothing. He just stared at the group at the table as if fascinated beyond speech.

The thin claw-like hand gradually came into view and Reiger, his mouth set in a hard grin, forced the hand on to the table. From where he stood, Fenner could see red-stained rags tied round each finger.

Carlos pushed a cheap pad of notepaper, a small bottle of ink and a brush towards the Chinese. 'Write,' he said.

The Chinese said nothing. He did nothing.

Carlos looked in Fenner's direction. 'Come here,' he said; 'I want you to see this.'

'I can see where I am,' Fenner said evenly.

Carlos shrugged. He picked up the object that he had taken from the drawer and carelessly fitted it on to one of the man's fingers.

Fenner turned his back slowly on the group and took Bugsey's arm. 'If you don't tell me what this means, I'm going to stop it,' he said hoarsely.

Bugsey's face was like green cheese. He said, 'The old guy's got three sons in his home town. Carlos wants him to send for them, to hook them up in his racket. Those three guys are worth four grand a head to Carlos.'

A sudden exclamation came from the other end of the room. Fenner turned his head. The Chinese was writing. Carlos got to his feet, his dull eyes watching every stroke of the pen. When the letter was finished the man fell back in the chair.

Carlos put his hand inside his coat and pulled a .25. He took a quick step towards the Chinese, put the muzzle of the gun at the back of his head and squeezed the trigger. The crash of the gun sounded incredibly loud in the silent room.

Carlos put his gun away and walked over to the table. He picked up the letter, folded it carefully and put it in his wallet.

'Tell Nightingale to get rid of him,' he said to Reiger, then walked directly over to Fenner. He stood and looked at Fenner narrowly. 'Now do you like my racket?' he said.

Fenner itched to get his hands on him. He said very gently, 'Maybe you've got a reason, but right now I think it's a little too tough.'

Carlos laughed. 'Come upstairs. I'll tell you about it.'

The coffee-shop had an air of reality, not like the room downstairs that gave Fenner the jitters. He sat down at a small table in a corner and took three quick deep breaths of hot air. Carlos sat down opposite him. Bugsey and Reiger went out and disappeared down the street.

Carlos pulled out a pouch and began to roll a cigarette. The tobacco was stringy and yellow-brown. A mulatto girl with enormous eyes brought two small cups of very strong black coffee. When she had gone, Carlos said:

'You're in this game now. If you don't like it, say so, and you can get out. If you want to go ahead, I'll tell you how it works. Once you know how it works, you'll have to stay in. Get the idea?' He smiled bleakly.

Fenner nodded. 'I'm stickin',' he said.

Carlos said, 'Don't rush it. A guy who knows too much about my affairs is likely to run into a lot of grief if he wants to get out sudden.'

'What have you gotta worry about? If I don't like it, that's my funeral.'

Carlos sipped his coffee and stared across the café with blank eyes. Then he said abruptly: 'There's a big demand on the West Coast for cheap Chinese labour. When I say cheap, I mean cheap. The authorities look on Chinks as undesirables, so they won't let them in. Now, that's a cock-eyed way of doin' things. The demand's there, but the guys who want them can't get them. Well, that's my racket. I get 'em in.'

Fenner nodded. 'You mean you smuggle them in?'

'It's easy. On this coast there are hundreds of places I can get them in. The coastguards don't give me no trouble. Sometimes I'm unlucky, but I get along.'

Fenner scratched his head. 'There ain't any dough in this line, is there?'

Carlos showed his teeth.

'You ain't quite got the angle,' he said. 'Look at it this way. First, the Chinks are crazy to get in here. I've got a guy in Havana who contacts them. They pay him to smuggle them across the Gulf. These Chinks are so hot to get in that they'll pay as much as five hundred to a thousand dollars. We take a load of twelve Chinks at a time. Once those guys have got on one of my boats and have coughed up the dough, they become my property. I see them to the West Coast, and a good Chink will fetch again as much as five hundred bucks.'

Fenner frowned.

'You mean the Chinks pay to get in, then you sell them once they're in?'

Carlos nodded.

'That's it,' he said. 'A two-way pay-off. It's quite a game. I've shipped fifty Chinks over this week. Taking everything into consideration, I'll pick up around thirty grand for that bit of work.'

This quite startled Fenner. He said: 'But why in hell don't these Chinks squawk? What happens to them?'

'How can they squawk? They got no right to be here. They can't go to the cops. It'd mean jail and bein' deported again. We send them up the coast and they get their food and that's all. You can find 'em workin' everywhere. In wash places, restaurants, laundries, everywhere.'

'Why did you want the old guy to write that letter?'

Carlos looked at him 'I'm tellin' you quite a lot, ain't I?'

Fenner met his glance. 'Be your age. You don't have to worry what you tell me.'

'That old guy's got three sons in China. We ain't gettin' enough Chinks over. I got him to write to his sons askin' 'em over. You know the stuff, sellin' them the idea of what a grand time he's havin' and what a lot of dough he's makin'. They'll come all right. Those Chinks are suckers for that stuff.'

Fenner pushed back his chair. 'Where do I come in?' he said.

'Maybe you'd like a trip over the Strait and collect some cargo for me. I'm sendin' over in a day or so.'

Fenner nodded. 'Sure, I'll do that,' he said. 'I'll look in each day. Your joint's a little too elaborate for me. It makes me feel coy. I guess I'll stick to the Haworth for a while.'

Carlos shrugged. 'Suit yourself,' he said; 'Bugsey'll keep in touch with you.'

Fenner nodded and pushed back his chair. 'Sure,' he said.

He went out into the street, leaving Carlos still sitting at the table.

Bugsey suddenly appeared from nowhere and tagged along behind Fenner. Fenner turned his head, saw him and stopped. Bugsey drew up with him, and they went on together.

Fenner said, 'Quite a racket, ain't it?'

Bugsey nodded. 'It's all right if you're some big-shot,' he said, without enthusiasm. 'I ain't gettin' places.'

Fenner looked at him sideways, thoughtfully. 'Ain't you gettin' anything out of this?'

'Sure, sure,' Bugsey said hastily. 'I'm not grumblin'.'

They wandered along the waterfront. Fenner thought this guy looked simple. He began to get ideas. He said, 'What's your rake-off?'

Bugsey said, 'A hundred bucks.'

'That's chicken-feed.'

'Sure, but it's tough these days.'

Fenner agreed that it was.

They moved along the waterfront idly watching the shipping. Fenner paused suddenly. He regarded a large luxury motor-launch that was lying off the short jetty. He said, 'Swell boat.'

Bugsey screwed up his eyes. 'Yeah,' he said wistfully. 'I'd like a tub like that.'

Fenner looked at him curiously. 'What in hell would you do with it, anyway?' he asked.

Bugsey heaved a sigh. 'Me? I'd get a flock of dames an' I'd take 'em out in that tub. That's what I'd do.'

Fenner wasn't listening to him, he was staring at a girl who had come up from the big cabin. She was a red-gold blonde with a neat figure, long legs, and long, narrow feet. She wore white trousers, red sandals and a red high-necked jersey. Fenner felt a little prickle of excitement. He knew who she was. He could see the points of likeness. This was Marian Daley's sister.

Bugsey noticed her, too. He whistled softly. 'What a frill!' he said.

Fenner said, 'Know who she is?'

'Me? Don't make me laugh. Think I'd be standin' here if I did?' Bugsey looked at her wistfully.

Fenner didn't hear him. He saw the name on the boat, *Nancy W*, and he wandered on. 'Havin' you around cramps my style,' he said. 'Alone, I'd 've got to first base. A frill like that's class. She's got no time for hoods.'

Fenner led him to a bar. 'All the same, pal, I'm goin' to have a try,' he said.

When the barman came to take the order, Fenner said, 'That's a swell boat out there.'

The bartender stared vacantly out through the open door and nodded. 'What'll you have?' he said.

Fenner ordered two gin slings. When the bartender brought them back, he tried again. 'Who owns her?'

The bartender scratched his head. 'What boat is it?'

'*Nancy W*.'

'Sure, that's a swell boat. Thayler's the guy. He's gotta heap of jack.'

Bugsey sighed. 'You'd wantta heap of jack to make a dame like that.'

'Thayler? What's his line?' Fenner went on.

The bartender shrugged. 'Just spends dough. One of these rich playboys, I guess.'

'Does he live around here?'

'A guy don't want to live around here when he's got a boat like that, does he?'

Fenner lowered half the gin sling. 'Who's the dame?'

The barman grinned. 'I can't keep up with them,' he said. 'I guess that guy's got a contract with the authorities to test them.'

Bugsey said, 'That's a swell job. Maybe he could do with a little help.'

Fenner said, 'Where can you meet a guy like that?'

'Meet him? He gets about. He's out a lot at Noolen's Casino.'

'So Noolen's got a casino, eh?' Fenner said, looking at Bugsey.

Bugsey sneered. 'Noolen's the south end of a horse.'

Fenner put his glass down on the counter. 'I'm beginning to believe that,' he said, and, putting his hand under Bugsey's arm, he led him into the sunlight.

Noolen's casino was close to Ernest Hemingway's house at the corner of Olivia and Whitehead.

Fenner stopped his cab to get a look at the Hemingway house. Then he went on to the casino.

It was a hot evening, full of noise and river smells. The casino stood back in a landscape garden, with a half-circular drive leading to the big double front doors. Double porches and arched windows, fitted with yellow-slatted shutters, gave the big house a touch of distinction.

A lot of cars crawled up the drive, unloaded, and crawled on back to the street.

Fenner paid off his cab and wandered up the long flight of broad stone steps. The front doors were open, and he could see a brilliantly lighted lobby as he mounted.

There were two men standing by the door who looked at him hard. He put them down as Noolen's muscle men. He went on through the lobby into a big room where two tables were in action. He wandered around, keeping his eyes open and hoping to find the girl from the boat.

He hadn't been in the room five minutes before a short Cuban in evening dress came up to him. 'Mr. Ross?' he said politely.

'What of it?' Fenner said.

'Will you come into the office a moment?'

Fenner smiled. 'I'm here to enjoy myself,' he said. 'What do I want in your office?'

The two men who had been standing at the door suddenly moved through the crowd and stood each side of him. They smiled at him, but the smile didn't reach their eyes.

The Cuban said softly, 'You'd better come, I think.'

Fenner shrugged and moved with him. They crossed the room, went out into the lobby and into a small room on the left.

Noolen was walking up and down, his head on his chest, and a big cigar clamped between his teeth. He glanced up at Fenner as he came in.

The Cuban shut the door, leaving the other two men outside.

Fenner thought Noolen looked in better shape. He seemed cleaner and his tuxedo suited him.

Noolen said, 'What are you doin' here?'

'This is public, ain't it? What's bitin' you?'

'We don't have any of Carlos's mob in here.'

Fenner laughed. He went over and sat in a big leather armchair. 'Don't be a mug,' he said.

Noolen stood very still. 'You better get out an' stay out. . . .'

Fenner raised his hand. 'Send the monkey away – I want to talk to you.'

Noolen hesitated, then he gave a sign to the Cuban, who went out.

'You're not going to get anywhere being tough with Carlos,' Fenner said, stretching his long legs. 'Why don't you get wise to yourself?'

'What's your game?' Noolen said. 'There's something about you I don't like.'

Fenner said seriously, 'I don't know. But string along. If my bet comes right, I may have to bust this town wide open. To do it, I might want you. I don't like Carlos and I don't like his racket. I think I'll wash him up.'

Noolen laughed. 'You're crazy. Carlos's big enough to smear you.'

Fenner nodded. 'That's how it looks, but that isn't the way it'll pan out. You'd like to see that guy go, wouldn't you?'

Noolen hesitated, then nodded. 'Yeah,' he said; 'but he ain't goin' in my lifetime.'

Fenner studied the toes of his shoes. 'You got a mob if I wanted one?'

Noolen came and sat down. 'I've gotta mob,' he said cautiously, 'but they're not in the same class. They'd be scared to start anything.'

Fenner grinned. 'Not when Carlos starts to slip. That's when your mob's got to go to work.'

Noolen clasped his hands. There was a long silence while he brooded. Then he said, 'You're playin' a tricky game. Suppose I have a little talk with Carlos.'

Fenner shrugged. 'Why should you? You've got everything to gain by just sittin' tight waitin' for me to clean up the town.'

'Okay. Then go ahead. I'll come in when I see you gettin' somewhere. Don't think you're going to clean my territory, because you ain't. One move from you and I don't like, an' I'll clamp down on you.'

Fenner got to his feet. 'We won't worry about that for a little while,' he said. 'There'll be plenty of time to take care of that angle later.'

Noolen looked up at him suspiciously. 'I don't trust you, Ross, you're too cagey.'

'Who's Thayler?' Fenner asked abruptly.

'Thayler? What's he to you?' Noolen's eyes were suddenly hot and intent.

'Saw his boat this afternoon. Swell job. Heard he came out here. Thought I'd like to look him over.'

Noolen got up and walked to the door. 'He's out there now.'

Fenner followed him into the main hall. 'Show him to me,' he said. 'I want to meet him.'

Noolen wandered through the crowd, looked right and left, then said, 'He's playin' on the third. The guy sittin' next to the blonde twist.'

Fenner saw the girl. She looked fine sitting there. The soft light reflected on her red-gold hair, making deep shadows of her eyes and making her red lips glisten. She was wearing a black dress that fitted her too well.

Fenner said, 'Who's the frill?' He said it very casually.

'Glorie Leadler. She's good, isn't she?' The blood had mounted in Noolen's face, and his blue eyes were watery. Fenner looked at him curiously. Noolen went on, 'You'll have to wait if you want to meet Thayler. He won't want to be interrupted.'

'That's all right. This Leadler girl, what is she?'

Noolen turned his head and looked at Fenner. 'Why the excitement?'

'Why not? She's a riot, ain't she?'

Noolen sneered. 'I'll leave you for a little while. I've got things to do,' he said, and walked away.

Fenner looked after him, wondered what it was all about, and walked over to the small bar at the other end of the room. He ordered a rye and ginger and leaned against the bar. From where he stood he could just see Glorie's head and shoulders. He looked at Thayler and studied him, a big man, with a very sunburnt complexion and black crinkly hair. His china-blue eyes and his long thin nose made him look handsome.

When Fenner glanced at Glorie again he found she was looking at him. Fenner regarded her thoughtfully, wondering at the uncanny likeness. If this dame wasn't Marian Daley's sister, then he was a three-legged horse.

Thayler leaned over a little and spoke to her, and she started. Fenner couldn't be sure, but he thought she had smiled at him. He thought maybe it had been a trick of the light, but it certainly had seemed that she'd given him a come-hither. He watched her closely, but she didn't look in his direction again. He stayed there for several minutes, then he saw her speak to Thayler and stand up. Thayler looked angry and put his hand on her wrist, but she shook her head, laughed at him and walked away from the table. Thayler screwed his head round to watch her, then turned back to the table again.

She came over to the bar. There were two other men standing close by, and the small Cuban manager. Fenner said, 'Drinking alone is a vice. Will you have one with me?'

She didn't look at him, but opened her small bag and took out a ten-dollar bill. 'I like vice,' she said softly, and ordered a gin sling. She stood with her back three-quarters to him. He could just see the lobe of her ear and the strong line of her chin.

Fenner finished his rye and ginger quickly and signalled the bartender for another. He studied her back thoughtfully, wondering. When the bartender put his order down on the polished wood, and had gone away, he said, 'Miss Leadler, I want to talk to you.'

She turned her head. 'Me?'

'Yeah. That's your name, ain't it?'

'Yes.' Her gaze began to embarrass him. He had a sudden uncomfortable feeling that she was seeing through him. No one had ever given him that feeling before. It confused him.

'My name's Ross. I'm staying at the Haworth. I want –' He broke off. Thayler was coming over fast. A heavy scowl darkened his face, and he came up to the bar with long quick strides. He said to Glorie, 'For God's sake, can't you just drink?'

Glorie laughed at him. She said in a clear voice, 'I think he's marvellous. I think he's absolutely, incredibly marvellous.'

Thayler looked uneasily at Fenner. 'Cut it out, Glorie,' he said under his breath.

She went on. 'He's the most beautiful thing I've seen. Look at his arms. Look at the size of them. Look at the set of his neck – the way he holds his head.'

Fenner took out his handkerchief and wiped his hands. He

finished his drink. The Cuban manager was watching him, a cold look of contempt on his face.

Thayler said savagely, 'You don't have to rave about his arms or his neck.'

'Ask him to have a drink. He's cute. Do you know what he said to me? He said, "Drinking alone's a vice." ' Glorie turned her head and smiled at Fenner.

Thayler said to Fenner, 'Get out of here, you.'

Glorie giggled. 'Be friendly. You're making him embarrassed. That's no way to talk to a lovely man like that.'

Fenner said, 'Watch yourself, playboy! You're a little too soft to talk big.'

Thayler made a move, but the Cuban manager slid between them. He said something to Thayler in a low voice. Thayler looked at Fenner over the top of the Cuban's head, his face was flushed with suppressed rage; then he turned, took Glorie by the wrist and walked out of the room.

Fenner said to the Cuban, 'Nice girl.'

The Cuban said, 'Maybe you'd better go, too,' and turned away.

Fenner stood thinking, then he snapped his fingers and left. He ran through the lobby, out into the black night. A cab shot up to the entrance and the driver swung the door open. Fenner said, 'Waterfront, fast,' and climbed into the cab.

Although the cab went fast, Thayler was already on board the *Nancy W.* when Fenner arrived. Fenner saw the light in the cabin flash as he paid off the cab driver. He looked hastily up and down the deserted waterfront, then ran along the jetty and climbed on board. Moving quietly, he reached the cabin. By lying full length, he could look down through the glass panel, which was half open.

Glorie was standing in the middle of the cabin, rubbing her wrist and looking at Thayler, who was leaning against the door. 'It's time we had a showdown,' he said. His voice came quite clearly to Fenner. 'I've been a sucker long enough.'

Glorie turned her back on him. 'Once I get out of here,' she said unevenly, 'I never want to see you again.'

Thayler went over to the sideboard and poured himself a drink. His hands shook so that the liquor slopped on the polished surface. 'I've done a hell of a lot for you,' he said. 'It's always the same. I know you're crazy, but can't you try? That's what gets me, you don't even try.'

Glorie moved round the room. She reminded Fenner of a caged animal.

'I'm sorry for you,' Thayler said.

She spun round. 'You're crazy. Do you think your sorrow means anything to me?'

'No one's sorrow has ever meant anything to you. You haven't any feeling, anyway.'

'Yes, I have.'

'Not that sort of feeling.'

Thayler held the glass in his hand very tightly. Fenner could see his knuckles were white. 'After this, I'm through with you. I'm not going to have another evening like this one.'

Glorie laughed suddenly. 'I'm sending you away, not you sending me. Shall I tell you why?'

'I'm sick of hearing it. I know it backwards.'

Glorie said spitefully, 'No, you don't. It's because you're no good. You were never any good. You're a flop. You don't know anything. You only think you do.'

Thayler put his glass carefully on the table. He walked over to her, and put his hands on her shoulders. His face was white. 'You know that's a damn lie, don't you?' he said.

She flung his hands off. 'I've got through telling lies to you, Harry,' she said. 'It isn't fun any more. One time I'd've let you keep your silly little pride. I can't be bothered now.'

Thayler smacked her face.

Fenner pushed his hat to the back of his head and moved a little further forward.

Thayler said in a trembling voice, 'I'll kill you for that.'

Glorie felt her cheek. 'You haven't the nerve to kill a rumour,' she snapped back. 'Don't you get tired using your head as a hat stand? Why don't you get wise? I'm through with you. I'm giving you the air.'

Thayler went very white. 'It's this other guy, huh?' he said. His hand touched the glass and he picked it up.

'Go easy with your blood pressure,' Glorie sneered, 'or you'll bust something.'

As she opened the door, Thayler flung the glass at her. It splintered against the wall a yard from her head.

Fenner drew away from the cabin skylight and stood up. 'Let 'em fight,' he thought, and, turning, he went away from the boat, heading towards his hotel.

Chapter Three

Fenner was in Nightingale's workroom, watching the little man staining a box when Reiger came in.

Reiger said, 'We got a job for you. I'll pick you up here at eight o'clock.'

Fenner lit a cigarette. 'What's the job?'

'You'll see.'

'Listen, Reiger. You ain't gettin' that way with me. Either you work with me or to hell with it. What's the job?'

Reiger scratched the side of his mouth with his thumbnail. 'We've got a consignment of Chinks. We're bringin' them over tonight.'

Fenner said, 'Okay, I'll be here.'

Reiger went out.

'Friendly guy that,' Fenner said to Nightingale. 'Somehow, I don't think he an' I hit it off.'

Nightingale looked worried. 'You're handlin' that guy wrong,' he said, shaking his head. 'He's mean. You'd better watch him.'

Fenner drummed on the top of a coffin-lid with his fingers. 'I'll watch him all right,' he said. He nodded to Nightingale and went downstairs. Curly was sitting at the desk writing in a ledger. She looked up hopefully as he went past.

Fenner paused. 'Hyah, baby,' he said. 'That's a nice face and figure you're wearin' this mornin'.'

Curly opened her big eyes. 'Gee!' she said. 'I don't get much of that syrup.'

'Never mind. It comes as a nice surprise when you do.'

Curly nibbled the top of her pen. She looked at him with thoughtful eyes. 'You're in this now?' she said.

Fenner nodded.

'Seen Pío?'

'I've seen him.'

Curly sighed. 'Ain't he a beautiful guy?'

'I wouldn't call him that. You don't think a lot of him, do you?'

Curly said bitterly, 'What does it matter what I think?'

Fenner had a sudden idea. He sat on the edge of her desk. 'Wait a minute, baby, don't get that way. Carlos mean anythin' to you?'

Curly said, 'No guy means anything to me. You keep your nose out of my business, will you?' Her eyes told him quite a lot.

He stood up and grinned. 'Sure, sure,' he said. 'Don't get me wrong. I thought maybe you'd like to put your curly little head on my shoulder an' tell me all your troubles.'

'Well, you're wrong,' she snapped. 'I've got no troubles.'

Fenner grinned again and went into the street. So that's the way it is, he thought. Curly had gone soft on Carlos and was getting nowhere. It was tough to fall for a little rat like Carlos.

He walked for some time through the narrow streets, retracing his steps, going into a bar for a short drink, and all the time checking to find out if anyone was tailing him. When he was satisfied no one was, he headed down-town again.

When he reached the Federal Building he loitered outside, keeping a close watch on the street; then he ducked into the building and took the elevator to the Federal Field Office.

The Federal Agent was named Hosskiss. He stood up behind his desk and offered a moist hand.

Fenner shook hands and sat down heavily in the chair opposite Hosskiss. He took some papers out of his inside pocket and handed them over. 'The name's Fenner. Here's my licence that permits me to operate as a private investigator. I'm on business for a client down here, and I want you to know some facts.'

Hosskiss examined the papers, frowned, and then said, 'Fenner? You the guy who broke the Blandish kidnapping case?'

Fenner nodded.

'Well, that's fine,' Hosskiss grinned. 'I used to know Brennan. He told me all about it. Why, sure, if I can help you I'll be glad.'

'I can't give you all the facts, but I'm looking for a girl. Somehow or other Carlos is tied up to the business. I've got an introduction to Carlos which was a fake and I've got a hook-up with his gang. I want you to know about this because I don't want to run foul of your boys. Tonight I'm going with Reiger to collect a cargo of Chinks. We are due to leave around eight o'clock. I thought maybe you'd like to hear about that.'

Hosskiss blew out his cheeks.

'Hell,' he said, 'you don't seem to know what sort of an outfit you're bucking. Listen, if Carlos hears about this you'll be cat's meat. That guy is the most dangerous rat on the coast.'

Fenner shrugged.

'I know that,' he said. 'I was careful. I don't think anyone spotted me coming here. Why haven't you clamped down on that gang?'

'No evidence. We know what his game is, but we've never caught him at it. We've got aeroplanes and boats watching the coast, but he seems to slip through easily enough. Once we did catch up with him, but he hadn't anythin' on board. They're a tough gang. I'm betting they dumped the aliens overboard as soon as they saw our boat heading towards them.'

Fenner scratched his head. 'If you catch up on us tonight you've got to let me out somehow. It's Reiger I'd like to see in a cage, but I've got to be in the clear so I can carry on with my investigation.'

Hosskiss said, 'I'll fix that for you. You wouldn't like to tell me what it's all about?'

Fenner shook his head. 'Not right now,' he said cautiously. 'I guess maybe I'll need your help for the final clean-up, but all I want now is for you to keep me in the clear if trouble comes my way.' He stood up.

Hosskiss shook hands. 'You don't know your course for to-night?'

Fenner shook his head. 'No,' he said; 'you'll have to find us.'

'We'll find you all right. I'll have the Strait lousy with boats.'

Out in the street again Fenner went on to the waterfront and picked up Bugsey. They went up to the Flagler Hotel.

Carlos was by himself when they entered No. 47. He nodded to them. He said to Bugsey, 'Go outside and rest yourself.'

Bugsey looked surprised, but he went out. Carlos looked at Fenner. Then he said, 'Why did you go to Noolen's joint the other night?'

Fenner said, 'I'm workin' for your mob, but I don't have to play with them, do I?'

Carlos said, 'You didn't play. You went into Noolen's office – why?'

Fenner thought quickly. Carlos was standing very still, his hand hovering near the front of his coat. 'I did go in to play, but Noolen sent for me an' told me to clear out. He didn't want any of your mob in his joint,' Fenner said.

Carlos said, 'You tried to talk with the Leadler woman – why?'

'Why not?' Fenner thought this was getting on dangerous ground. 'Any guy would try for a frill like that. She was on her own, so I thought we might get friendly. What do you know about her?'

Carlos's eyes snapped. 'Never mind about that. I don't like the way you're acting, Ross. Both those stories come too easy. I think I'll watch you.'

Fenner shrugged. 'You're losing your nerve,' he said contemptuously. 'You ain't scared of Noolen?'

Carlos jerked his head. 'You can go,' he said, and walked to the window.

Fenner went out thoughtfully. This guy wasn't such a dope as he'd thought. He would have to play his cards carefully. He said to Bugsey, 'I'll be with you in a second. I wantta 'phone my hotel an' tell 'em I won't be in tonight.'

He shut himself in a booth and called Noolen. Bugsey hung about outside. Fenner said, keeping his voice low, 'Noolen? Ross speakin'. Listen, Carlos has got a plant at your gambling house. He knew you an' me had a talk, and he knew other things. That Cuban manager of yours – had him long?'

'Two months.' Noolen's voice sounded worried. 'I'll check up on him.'

'Yeah,' said Fenner grimly, 'I'd get rid of that guy quick,' and he hung up. He walked out of the booth and took Bugsey's arm. 'We'll go an' take things easy,' he said. 'Looks like I'll have a little hard work tonight.'

Bugsey went with him. He said in a low, confidential voice, 'I gotta date myself.' He closed his eyes and smiled.

Fenner showed at Nightingale's two minutes before eight. Reiger and Miller were already there. Miller was greasing a sub-machine-gun. They both looked up as Fenner followed Nightingale into the workroom.

Fenner said, 'I smell rain.'

Reiger grunted, but Miller said in a false, friendly way, 'That's what we want, rain.'

Nightingale said to Fenner in a low voice, 'You got a rod?'

Fenner shook his head.

Nightingale went over to a drawer and took out a big automatic. Reiger jerked up his head. 'He don't want a rod.'

Nightingale took no notice. He handed the gun to Fenner. Reiger seemed to get quite excited. 'I tell you he don't want a rod,' he said, standing up.

Fenner looked at him. 'Give it a haircut,' he said. 'I feel safer with a rod.'

They stared at each other, then Reiger shrugged and sat down again.

Nightingale gave a peculiar smile. 'You given up packing a rod?' he said to Fenner. 'They tell me you're dynamite with a trigger.'

Fenner balanced the automatic thoughtfully in his hand. 'I get by,' was all he said.

Miller looked at the small watch that seemed out of place on his thick wrist. 'Let's go,' he said. He wrapped the machine-gun in his dust-coat and picked up his hat.

Reiger moved to the door. Nightingale said softly to Fenner: 'Watch those two birds.'

There was a big sedan parked outside the Funeral Parlour. Reiger got under the driving-wheel, and Fenner and Miller got in behind. Fenner waved his hand to Nightingale as the car slid away. He caught a glimpse of Curly watching behind Nightingale. He could just make out the blurred outline of her face.

He said to Miller: 'Carlos never comes on these runs, does he?'

'Why should he?' Miller said shortly.

Reiger swung the car south. 'You're always askin' questions, ain't you?' he said.

They rode the rest of the way in silence. When they got down to the waterfront they left the car parked and walked rapidly down to the line of small shipping. A tall Negro and Bugsey were waiting alongside a forty-foot boat. As soon as the Negro saw them coming he climbed aboard and disappeared into the engine-room. Bugsey stood ready to cast off.

Reiger said, while Miller climbed aboard, 'You don't do anythin' until they come alongside. Then you gotta watch them as they come aboard. Not one of these Chinks must have guns. The safest way to deal with them is to make them strip as they come on board. It takes time, but it's safe. If you think one of them's got a rod, take it off him. If he looks like startin' anything, give it to him. Miller will take them from you and put them in the forward cabin.'

Fenner said, 'Sure,' and followed Reiger on board. Bugsey cast off and tossed the bowline to Reiger. He waved his hand to Fenner. 'Nice trip,' he said.

The Negro started the engines and the boat began to shudder

a little. Miller was already down in the cockpit, his hand on the wheel.

Reiger said, 'All right – let her go,' and the boat began to show her heels.

Reiger went over to the small but powerful searchlight on the foredeck. He squatted down behind it and lit a cigarette. His back was intent and unfriendly, and Fenner didn't bother to follow him. He climbed down into the cockpit with Miller and made himself comfortable.

'What time will you pick these guys up?' he asked Miller.

'Around about ten, I guess.'

As the boat headed for the open sea, it grew suddenly chilly and a drizzling rain began to fall. There was no moon and the visibility was bad.

Fenner shivered a little and lit a cigarette. Miller said, 'You get used to these trips. If you feel cold go into the engine-room. It'll be warmer there.'

Fenner stayed with Miller a little longer, then he went off to the engine-room. He noticed Reiger still sitting behind the searchlight, immovable.

The boat bounced a good bit in the rough, and Fenner suddenly lost interest in smoking. The Negro didn't say a word. Now and then he rolled his eyes at Fenner, but he didn't say anything.

After some time Miller yelled and Fenner joined him. Miller pointed. An intermittent flash of light came from a long way off. Miller had altered the course and the boat was running directly toward the light. 'I guess that must be our man,' he said.

Reiger suddenly switched on his searchlight, and almost immediately he snapped it off again.

Very faintly Fenner heard the drone of an aeroplane. He smiled in the darkness. Miller heard it, too. He bawled to Reiger, 'There's a plane coming.'

Reiger stood up and looked up into the blackness overhead. Then he hurriedly put out the running lights. The boat went on through the curtain of blackness.

Miller said savagely, 'Those coastguards give me a pain.'

The aeroplane droned on, then, after a few minutes, faded away. Reiger flashed on the searchlight again, let the beam cut the darkness, and then turned it off. The other light kept on flickering. It was drawing nearer and nearer.

Miller handed Fenner a torch. 'Go forward,' he said; 'we're nearly there.'

Fenner took the torch and climbed out of the cockpit. He felt the boat roll as Miller cut speed.

Reiger, who was standing well forward, shouted, 'Kill it,' and with a flurry the engines stopped. Reiger came over to Fenner, walking carefully as the boat rolled and heaved. 'Get your rod out,' he snapped, 'and watch these guys.' He was holding the sub-machine-gun. 'I'll pass them to you. Make sure they ain't got guns, then pass them to Miller.'

They both stared into the inky blackness. Reiger flashed on a small torch suddenly. He had heard the creak of oarlocks.

A small rowboat came bobbing towards them. Fenner could see four men huddled in it and two men at the oars, then Reiger put his lamp out.

'Keep your ears back for that aeroplane,' Reiger muttered to Fenner. Then, as the rowboat bumped gently alongside, he put his lamp on again.

A thin scraggy Chinaman came aboard. 'I got four here,' he said to Reiger. 'I'll bring the others in four lots.'

'What about the special?'

'Sure, sure, I'll bring the special last.'

Reiger said to Fenner. 'Okay, let's start.'

Fenner stepped back and waited. The Chinese came on board one by one. Reiger counted them, letting only one come at a time, waiting for Fenner to pass them to Miller, who directed them to the forward cabin. Each Chinese wore the same clothes, tight shirts and knee-length trousers. They stood sheep-like before Fenner, who patted them down and shoved them over to Miller.

Two more boatloads came out and it all took some time. The scraggy Chinese who had stood on the right-hand side of Reiger while this was going on, said, 'Okay, that's the lot. I'll go back for the special now.'

Reiger said to Miller, 'You locked those Chinks in?' His voice sounded uneasy to Fenner.

'Bolts on,' Miller assured him.

Fenner wondered what the 'special' was. He sensed a sudden tension between Miller and Reiger. They all waited in the darkness, their ears straining for the long-boat to return. At last they heard the faint splash of oars. Reiger snapped on his torch and, reaching out with a boat-hook held the long-boat steady.

The scraggy Chinese climbed on board. He reached down and the oarsman handed a small figure over to him. A quick pull, and the special was aboard.

'Don't you worry about this,' Reiger said to Fenner.

Fenner flashed his torch on the special. He gave a soft grunt. It was a girl. He'd guessed as much. She was about thirteen or fourteen years old, Chinese, and pretty. She looked very scared and cold. She wore the same tight shirt and knee-length trousers.

With an oath Reiger struck the torch from his hand. 'Keep out of this,' he said between his teeth. 'Miller, get her under cover.'

Reiger turned to the Chinese, who gave him a package wrapped in oilskin, and then climbed into the long-boat which disappeared into the night.

Fenner said between his teeth: 'There's a nice rap hanging to this sort of racket.'

Reiger said, 'Yeah? You gettin' milky?'

'I guess I was entitled to know you were runnin' women. That ain't a thing that gets passed over easily.'

'What do you think? A twist is worth ten Chinks, if you can get them. So shut up, will you?'

Fenner didn't say anything, he let Reiger go to the cockpit. He stood there brooding. Was this the answer to the riddle? They'd picked up twelve Chinks and a woman. Was that what this sister of Marian's was trying to hint at? Or was it just a coincidence? He didn't know.

Miller shouted. 'Take her back, Reiger, I've had enough of it.'

Reiger said, 'Sure, tell the Nigger to start her up.'

The boat quivered as the engines sprang into life. Fenner sat down with his back to the cockpit roof and searched the darkness. His ears strained, hoping to pick up the sound of a patrol boat. He neither heard nor saw anything.

Reiger shouted suddenly. 'Ross – where the hell are you? Hi, Ross!'

Fenner dropped into the cockpit. 'What's the matter?' he said. 'Scared of the dark?'

'Listen, bright boy, suppose you lay off the funny angle? I want you to go into the Chinks' cabin and chain them together. There are the chains over there.'

Fenner looked at the heap of handcuffs linked together with rusty chains that lay in the corner. 'What for?' he said.

'What you think? We gotta be careful, ain't we? If a patrol boat gets on our tail we shove the rats over. Chained like that they go down quick.'

Fenner said, 'The things you think of!' He took the wheel out of Reiger's hand. 'Do it yourself. That ain't up my street.'

Reiger looked at him in the dim light of the navigation lamp. 'Somehow I don't think you're goin' to be a lotta use with our mob,' he said, and picking up the chains, he climbed out of the cockpit and disappeared.

Fenner made a little face. He couldn't see how much longer he was going to keep this up. He was nearly satisfied that he'd got as much information as he wanted. It depended on what this Glorie Leadler would have to say. If he got what he hoped from her, then he could strike and wash the whole business up.

A muffled sound of a gun going off jerked his attention to the boat again. He listened, peering ahead but seeing nothing. There was silence, and after a little while Reiger came back into the cockpit again.

Fenner glanced at him as Reiger took the wheel from him. Reiger's face was hard and cold. 'Trouble?' Fenner said.

Reiger grinned. 'They don't like the chains. I had to shoot one of the punks in the leg before they'd quiet down.'

Fenner ran his hand through his hair. It had stopped raining, but he felt cold and damp.

'Go along an' tell Miller to watch that broad,' Reiger said suddenly. 'She looked quiet, but if she starts a squeal, there'll be hell on this ship.'

Fenner went aft to the small cabin behind the galley. He walked into the cabin and stopped. Miller was struggling with the Chinese girl. She fought him silently, blood running from her nose and from her lips.

Fenner took a step forward and grabbed Miller by his collar. He heaved, dragging Miller away from the girl. When he got him clear, he booted him hard, sending him sprawling to the other side of the small cabin.

Miller sat up slowly. His great white face glistened in the lamplight. He focused on Fenner by screwing up his eyes.

'Get out of here, an' leave me alone,' he said thickly.

Fenner didn't say anything. He just stood, his hands hanging loose at his side. Miller looked round the cabin, saw the girl, and scrambled over to her.

Fenner, white-faced and thin-lipped, slid his gun so that he held it by the short barrel. He sucked in his breath and hit Miller on the top of his head. Miller stiffened, went limp. He twitched once, as if trying to command his muscles, then his forehead hit the floor with a little thud.

Fenner shoved his gun away and took him by his arm and dragged him out of the cabin.

Reiger shoved his head over the top of the cockpit. 'What the hell's goin' on?' he shouted.

Fenner took no notice. He dumped Miller in the scuppers.

Miller sat up, holding his head. He mumbled a hoarse stream of obscenities. Fenner didn't look at him; he went over to the cockpit and climbed down.

Reiger said, 'What's goin' on?'

Fenner had difficulty in keeping his voice steady. 'That heel Miller was after the girl. I bounced him.'

Reiger shrugged. 'You should worry about her.'

Fenner didn't answer. He was looking at a tiny moving light on their port side. He hastily looked away before Reiger noticed. He wondered if it were a patrol boat.

Miller, who had staggered to his feet, saw it and yelled a warning. Reiger looked and spun the wheel.

'Coastguards,' he said; 'maybe they won't spot us.'

The boat was still running without lights, but the moon had climbed above the belt of clouds, and the big white wash showed up pretty well.

Fenner watched the light, saw it swing round a little and head towards them. He said gently, 'They've seen us all right.'

Reiger yelled for Miller. He gave the boat all the gas she'd take. Miller came staggering down into the cockpit. He glared at Fenner murderously, but Reiger snarled, 'Take the wheel. I'm gettin' the gun out. Maybe this guy's faster'n us.'

Miller took the wheel and Reiger disappeared aft. Fenner climbed out of the cockpit and followed Reiger. The light was coming up now, and as the moonlight began to flood the sea, Fenner could make out the boat. It was fast all right. He could see the way the bows were lifted right out of the water.

He said to Reiger, 'This boat's goin' to catch us.'

Reiger shouted down into the engine-room, and the Negro handed up a Thompson gun. Reiger gave it to Fenner, and took another from the Negro.

'You get on the port side,' Reiger said, lying down flat. 'Keep firing at them.'

Fenner lay down. He fired two bursts, taking care that the bullets would go well over the top of the boat. Almost immediately, Reiger fired with his gun. Even from where he lay, Fenner could see a shower of white splinters spurt from the bows of the oncoming boat.

Fenner ducked his head as the coastguards replied. He saw the long yellow flashes and heard the thud of bullets as they bit into the sides of the boat. The coastguards kept up such a heavy fire that it was impossible for either Reiger or Fenner to show themselves to fire back.

Miller, watching from the cover of the cockpit, screamed out, 'Do somethin'. They'll be up in a few seconds.'

Reiger peered from behind his cover, saw the boat was within six feet or so and ducked back as the wood began to splinter again.

Fenner turned his head. He could see Reiger lying flat. Reiger shouted to him, 'Stand by for a headache,' and leaning over on his side he tossed a small ball-like object right into the other boat.

There was a blinding flash and a violent explosion and the coastguard boat immediately began to fall astern.

'Keep her going,' Reiger shouted to Miller, and sat up to watch the coastguard boat burst into flames. He scrambled over to Fenner. 'That's the first time we've tried that stunt. Carlos's some guy with his ideas. If we hadn't had that pineapple on board the Chinks would be feedin' the fishes by now, an' we'd have had a lost journey.'

Fenner grunted. He couldn't take his eyes off the burning boat, which was rapidly becoming a little red glow in the darkness. He got slowly to his feet. Reiger had already gone forward. He was pointing to a green light that flickered in the distance. Miller swung the wheel a little.

'That's the guy who takes our load,' Reiger shouted to Fenner. 'We've got through all right.'

Fenner stood watching the green light come nearer. He knew now that he must start things moving. He'd played with Carlos long enough.

It was just after two o'clock in the morning when Fenner got back to the Haworth. Before he switched on his room light he knew someone was there. He didn't hear anything, but he knew he wasn't alone. He stepped inside, feeling uncomfortably exposed in the dimly lighted doorway. There was something in the air, a scent. He reached inside his coat and pulled his gun, then he groped for the wall switch and flicked the light on.

A woman's clothes on the floor at the foot of his bed caught his eye. A black dress, a handful of lace and crêpe de chine, a pair of shoes.

Glorie Laidler sat up in his bed. Two bare arms curved up over the sheet, holding the sheet firmly against her body. When she saw who it was, she lay back again, keeping her arms out and arranging her red-gold hair on Fenner's pillow.

Fenner put his gun away. The only thing he could think of was that he was tired and that he'd have to strip his bed when she had gone. He didn't fancy sleeping in the same sheets.

Glorie smiled at him sleepily.

Fenner went over to the floor lamp, put it on, and turned off the ceiling lamp. The light was softer, but it lit up the floor brightly. He saw two little red marks on his carpet which hadn't been there before. He looked at the red marks and then he looked at Glorie's shoes. He moved further into the room. There were red marks on the shoes, as if Glorie had stepped in something. Without picking the shoes up, Fenner couldn't be sure. He knew pretty well the marks were bloodstains, but he didn't want her to know he'd seen them just yet.

Fenner said, 'Why have you come here?'

'It's you. You said Haworth. You said you wanted to talk. I came here and waited. I got tired of waiting, so I got into bed. I thought you wouldn't come back tonight.'

'When did you come here?'

'What do you mean – when?' Her slatey eyes went a little cold.

'What time?'

'Nine o'clock. I waited until eleven and then I came to bed.'

'Anyone see you come in?'

She shook her head. Fenner thought she had gone a little white. She moved restlessly in the bed. He could see the long outline of her legs under the thin sheet. A lot of the bravado had gone out of her. She said, 'You sound like a big policeman askin' nasty questions.'

Fenner smiled bleakly. 'Just rehearsing you, baby,' he said. 'You haven't much of an alibi, have you?'

Glorie sat up in bed. She said, 'What – what are you saying?'

Fenner shook his head. 'Get under cover. You're too big a girl for this sort of thing now.'

She pulled the sheet up over her, but she didn't lie down. 'What do you mean – alibi?'

He reached over and picked up one of her shoes. He examined it carefully. The sole was covered with dry blood. He tossed the shoe in her lap. She gave a husky little scream and threw it from her. Then she lay back, put her hands over her face and began to cry.

Fenner went to a cupboard, took out a bottle of Scotch and gave himself a drink.

He lit a cigarette and took off his hat and coat. It was very hot and close in the room. He walked over to the open window and looked into the deserted street. 'You'd better tell me,' he said.

She said, 'I don't know anything about it.'

He wandered back to the bed and sat down. 'Then the quicker you get out of this room the better pleased I'll be. I don't want to be dragged into a murder rap.'

She said, between choking sobs: 'I found him. He was lying on the floor. Someone had shot him.'

Fenner ran his fingers through his hair. 'Who?' he said gently.

'Harry – Thayler, the man I was with.'

Fenner brooded. 'Where is he?' he said at last.

Glorie took her hands away. Fenner experienced a little shock. She certainly wasn't crying. She was play-acting. She said, 'On his boat.'

'When did you find him?'

'Just before I came to you.'

Fenner rubbed his eyes. He got up and put his coat and hat on again. 'Wait here,' he said. 'I'm goin' down to have a look at him.'

She said, 'I'll come with you.'

Fenner shook his head. 'You keep out of this. Stay here. When I get back I want to talk to you.'

Then he went out of the room and down to the waterfront.

He found *Nancy W* and climbed on board. He went down into the main cabin. It was dark and he couldn't find Thayler. He searched the whole boat, but he couldn't find anything. He turned on the light in the sleeping cabin after closing the port-hole. From the clothes lying about, he thought this must be where Thayler had slept.

He went through the chest of drawers carefully.

The only thing he found which really astonished him was a small photo of Curly Robbins, taken, as far as he could judge, several years ago. He took the photo and put it in his wallet. Then he shut the drawer and snapped off the light.

He went back to the main cabin again and examined the carpet. It was only when he looked very closely that he could see that the carpet had been recently washed in one small patch. He stood up, scratching his head. He was quite certain now that Thayler was not on board.

Was Thayler dead? Could he rely on what Glorie had said? If he'd been killed, who had got rid of his body and washed up the carpet? Had Glorie killed him? The last time he'd seen those two together they weren't exactly acting friendly.

He said with exasperation, 'Nuts!' and went out of the cabin. As he stepped on the jetty he noticed a big sedan drawn up without lights on the other side of the waterfront. He gave it a quick look, and then dropped flat. A choked roar came from the car as he did so and he knew someone had let off a shot-gun in his direction. He pulled his gun and kept flat. He heard the car start and the swish of tyres on the sandy road. Then the car swept out of sight round the corner.

Fenner got up and dusted himself. Things were getting complicated. He walked back to the Haworth, keeping in the shadows and using the back streets only.

Glorie lay just where he had left her. Her face was a little pinched, and the smile she gave him was only a twist of the mouth.

He pulled up the chair again and sat down. 'Was he in the main cabin when you saw him?' he said abruptly.

She said, 'Yes.'

Fenner nodded, as if he expected that. 'They've taken him away now,' he said. 'I don't know why they did that, because if they wanted a fall-guy you'd've been it. Either you killed him and tossed him overboard or you didn't, and the killer came back for some reason or other and took him away. Maybe you tossed him overboard.'

Glorie showed her long arms. 'Do you think I could do it? He was big.'

Fenner thought of the almost perpendicular stairs leading into the cabin, and shook his head. 'No,' he said. 'I guess that's right.'

The colour came back to her face and she didn't look so drawn.

She said, 'If they hid him away, no one will know he's dead, will they?'

Fenner yawned. 'That's right,' he said.

She curled down in the bed, pulling the pillow off the bolster. 'Don't you think I look snug?' she said, her eyes getting flirtatious again.

Fenner said, 'Where's your sister Marian?'

She didn't jump more than an inch, but it looked like a couple of yards. Fenner leaned over her and pulled her round. Her eyes were startled. 'Where's your sister?' he repeated.

She said, 'What do you know about her? *How* do you know about her?'

Fenner sat down close to her. 'You're as like as two peas,' he said. 'I've never seen anything quite like it.' He put his hand inside his pocket and took out the letter he had found in Marian's bag. 'Look at that,' he said.

She read it through blankly, and then shook her head. 'I don't know,' she said. 'Who's Pío? Who's Noolen?'

Fenner went over to the table, picked up a pad of notepaper and a pencil and came back to the bed. 'Write that letter out for me,' he said.

As she struggled up, he said hastily, 'Wait.' He went to the cupboard and got his pyjama jacket and threw it over to her. Then he went into the bathroom and waited a few seconds. When he came out she had put the coat on and was rolling back the long sleeves.

She said, 'Why do you want me to do this?'

'Do it.' He spoke very curtly.

She scribbled on the pad and then gave it to him. He compared the two handwritings. There was nothing similar about them. He tossed the pad on the table again and began to walk up and down the room slowly. She watched him nervously.

'You've got a sister, haven't you?' he said at last.

She hesitated, then she said, 'Yes; but we haven't seen each other for a very long time.'

'How long? Why haven't you?'

'Four or five years, I forget exactly. Marian and I didn't get on so well. She'd got ideas about how I should live. We didn't quarrel, but she kept having ideas. So we split when father died.'

Fenner said gently, 'You're lying. If you hadn't seen each other for that length of time, why did she come to me all fussed because you were missing?'

Two little patches of red burnt in Glorie's cheeks. 'I didn't know she came to you. Who are you, anyway?'

'Never mind who I am. When did you last see Marian?'

Glorie looked sulky. 'I was in New York with Harry. We ran into each other. It was about a couple of weeks ago. I was up there on a trip. Marian wanted me to come to her hotel. I said I would, because she was so insistent. I had Harry with me. It was awkward. Marian wouldn't stand for Harry, so I gave her the slip and came back to Florida.'

Fenner came over and sat on the bed. 'Either you're telling a lot of lies, or else there's somethin' I've missed in all this,' he said.

Glorie shook her head from side to side. 'I'm not lying,' she said. 'Why should I?'

'Listen, did you say anything to your sister about twelve Chinese?'

'Twelve Chinese? Why should I?'

'Don't keep sayin' "Why should I?" ' Fenner said savagely. 'It confuses me.'

As far as he could see he was no further, now he'd met this girl, than he was before. He thought, and then said, 'Why Leadler? Why not Daley?'

'Leadler's my married name,' Glorie said. 'I was divorced a year ago.'

Fenner grunted. 'Where's your husband?'

She shook her head. 'I don't know,' she said. 'Why?'

Fenner didn't answer. Instead he said, 'Your sister was murdered last week in a house in Brooklyn.'

There was a long silence. Glorie said, 'I don't believe it.' Her eyes crawled up and down Fenner's face.

Fenner shrugged. 'You don't have to,' he said; 'but she was murdered all right. I liked that girl. She came to me for help. I didn't like the way she met her finish, an' I'm promising myself to fix the guy who killed her.'

Glorie took his coat in her hand. She twisted the coat and shook him. 'Marian dead?' she said. 'You sit there like that and say that to me? You haven't any pity for me! Marian – Marian –'

Fenner put his hand on her wrist and jerked her hand away. 'Cut it out,' he said. 'You can't act. You don't give a hoot what happened to Marian.'

Glorie looked at him and then giggled. She put her hand over her mouth and her eyes looked shocked. 'I shouldn't've done that,' she said. 'Fancy Marian getting murdered.' She rolled over in the bed and buried her face in the pillows. She began to shake with laughter.

Fenner had a sudden idea. He put his hand on her head, shoved her down into the pillow, and pulled down the sheet with his other hand. Still holding her, he jerked the pyjama jacket over her shoulders and looked carefully at her back. He pulled the jacket down and pulled up the sheet, then he stepped back.

Glorie twisted round, her eyes bright. 'Why – why did you do that?' she said.

'Did you know your sister had bruises all over her back?' Fenner said.

'You know everything, don't you?' and she began to cry. When Fenner saw the tears running from her eyes, he walked away to the window. He began to feel horribly tired. He said abruptly: 'I'll see more of you tomorrow,' and walked to the door. The sound of her sobbing followed him downstairs. He thought, 'I'll go crazy if somethin' doesn't happen soon,' and he went to the night clerk to arrange for another room.

The bright sunlight came through the slatted shutters and lay like prison bars across Fenner's bed.

He stirred restlessly as a clock downstairs faintly chimed ten. At the eighth chime he opened his eyes and grunted. His body still felt tired, and his head ached a little. He was dimly conscious of the sunlight, and he closed his eyes again. Then, as his mind struggled out of sleep he was aware of a weight at the foot of his bed and scent on the air. As he groaned, Glorie giggled. He looked at her through half-closed eyes, and his half-awakened senses said she looked very nice. She was curled up, with her back resting on the end of the bedstead, her long legs up to her chin, and her fingers laced round her knees. She rested her chin in the little hollow between her knees and regarded Fenner with bright eyes.

'When you're asleep you look kind and beautiful,' she said. 'Isn't that wonderful?'

Fenner struggled up in bed. He ran his fingers through his hair. He felt terrible.

'Would you mind goin' away?' he said patiently. 'When I want to see you I'll tell you. I dislike women in my bedroom on principle. I'm old-fashioned and I'm easily shocked.'

Glorie giggled. 'You're cute,' she said simply.

Fenner groaned. Now he was sitting up his head ached sharply. 'Run away,' he said. 'Beat it! Scram!'

Glorie threw her arms wide. Her incredibly blue eyes sparkled. 'Don't you like me? Don't you think I'm marvellous?' she said.

Fenner said unpleasantly, 'Will you run away?'

Glorie slid off the bed. She looked funny in Fenner's pyjamas. They hung on her like a sack.

Fenner said, 'Anyway, you look like something the cat dragged in. Why not go away and get dressed, then maybe we'll have breakfast and another talk.'

Glorie giggled and began dancing round the room. Fenner thought she was the most beautiful bit of corruption he'd ever seen.

She laughed at him. 'Say, you must like me!' she said.

Fenner sat up on his elbow. 'Go away,' he said shortly, 'I don't want to be bothered just now.'

She said, 'Do you really mean that?' Doubt had come into her eyes, like the slow movement of a cloud across the face of the moon. She came over to the bed and sat close to him.

Fenner nodded. 'Pull your freight, sister,' he said. 'I'll see you later.'

He thought for a moment that she was going to hit him. Then she got up and wandered out of the room, leaving the door open. Fenner got out of bed and kicked the door to, and went into the bathroom. He thought:

'What a hell of a note to start the morning on.' After a shower he felt better and he rang for coffee. He was dressed when the waiter brought up the coffee. Two cups put him right and he went along to Glorie's room. She was dressed. Her black evening dress looked out of place in the sunlight. She was sitting by the window looking into the street.

Fenner wandered in and shut the door softly behind him. He said, 'What are you going to do?'

Glorie turned and smiled at him. It was quite a shock. Her eyes were wide, candid and friendly. She said, 'What can I do?'

He leaned against the wall and stared at her thoughtfully.

He said at last, 'You're difficult to understand. I thought I was goin' to have a lot of trouble with you. I see I was wrong.'

She swivelled round, her back to the window. 'I still think you're cute,' she said. Then she added, 'I'm going to grow on you.'

Fenner's eyes shifted past her, looked into the street. A black sedan was standing below. He'd seen that car before. Even as he started forward a man's arm came through the curtained window. The sun reflected on a gun. That was the flash picture Fenner had, a picture that paralysed him, making him seconds late. He heard a faint *phut* as Glorie screamed. Not a loud scream – soft, hoarse. Then she bent at the knees. Before Fenner could do anything about it, she slid to the floor.

The sedan went away fast. It all happened at such an incredible speed that no one seemed conscious of it in the street. Fenner leaned out of the window, saw the sedan swing round the corner and disappear.

He stepped away and knelt down swiftly. As he turned Glorie, his right hand felt a wet patch on her side, just above her hip. She'd gone very white, but she was breathing. Fenner reached out and grabbed a cushion from a nearby chair and put it under her head. Then he ran into the bathroom. He filled a hand bowl with water, snatched up a small first-aid case he always kept with him and went back.

She watched him come across the room, her eyes wide with fear. She said, 'I can't feel anything. Am I badly hurt?'

Fenner knelt down. 'Take it easy,' he said. 'We'll look an' see.'

He opened the case and selected a scalpel. 'I guess your dress'll have to go,' he said, cutting the silk carefully.

She said, 'I'm glad I was with you,' and began to cry.

Fenner cut the top of her girdle. 'Keep yourself in hand,' he said, working quickly. 'The shock's bound to tilt you sideways.' He examined the wound, and then grinned. 'Well, I'll be dammed. It's only a nick. The slug's just made a groove in your side.'

She said, 'I was scared that I was going to die.'

'So was I.' Fenner fixed the wound with experienced fingers. 'All the same, that was nice shooting. That guy was some sniper.'

Glorie said in a small voice, 'It hurts now.'

'Sure, it's bound to hurt.' Fenner straightened and looked down at her. 'You'll have to lie up for a few days. Maybe that'll keep you out of mischief. I'm goin' to take you home. Where do you live?'

She looked away from him, her face suddenly blank, then she gave a little giggle that finished on a gasp of pain. 'I haven't got a home,' she said, putting her hand on her side.

'Where did you live before you threw in with Thayler?'

She looked at him sharply, then looked away again. 'I didn't throw in with Harry —'

Fenner knelt beside her. 'You're a rotten liar,' he said. 'You said last night you and Thayler were doing a trip to New York together. Now you say you didn't throw in with him. Give it to me straight.'

She said jerkily, 'I believe you're a detective.'

Fenner snorted. 'Listen, redhead, you can't lie about floors all day. I've gotta get you somewhere. Either you tell me where you live, or else I'll send for an ambulance.'

She said, 'I want to stay here.'

Fenner smiled unpleasantly. 'I'm not going to be your nurse-maid,' he said. 'I gotta lot to do.'

She said, 'I'm safer here.'

Fenner paused, thought, and then said, 'I see.' He went over to the bed and pulled the sheet down. Then he picked her up very gently, sitting her in a chair. She chewed her lip while he did this. He took the scalpel and cut the dress down each side.

She said, 'What a mess,' and went so white he thought she was going to faint.

'Hold it,' he said sharply, and stood her up. 'Get a grip on yourself.'

She put her face against his. 'You're cute,' she said in a small voice.

He jerked his head away. 'Cut it out!' he said, and carried her over to the bed. He was glad to get her covered up.

She lay with her red-gold head on the pillow and looked up at him. She looked suddenly very young and defenceless. She said, 'I want to whisper.'

Fenner shook his head. 'Try another one. That's got whiskers on it.'

She reached up her two arms. 'Please!'

He bent his head and she kissed him. Her lips felt very soft against his. It was just a youthful kiss, and Fenner quite liked it. He straightened and rumpled his hair. 'Take it easy,' he said. 'I'm going to fix things.' He pulled up the sheet to her chin, cleared her clothes and the rest of the mess into the bathroom, and went downstairs.

The hotel manager looked at him with an odd expression. Fenner felt a little embarrassed. He said, 'My girl friend's run into a little accident. She'll have to stay in bed. I want you to send someone out an' get her a sleeping suit an' whatever else she wants. Put it all on the bill.'

The manager said quite seriously, 'This is a little irregular –'

Fenner interrupted him. 'I'll say it's irregular,' he said shortly, 'but it ain't so irregular that it calls for a fan dance from you, so snap to it.'

He went over to a telephone booth and dialled a number. A hoarse voice floated over the wire.

'Bugsey?' Fenner asked. 'Listen, Bugsey. I gotta job for you. Yeah, just the job you've been wantin'. Come on over to my dump an' bring a rod.'

He went into the bar and ordered two fingers of rye. He felt he wanted a drink after all the excitement. While he waited for Bugsey he remembered something. He took out his wallet. When he opened the wallet a frown came to his eyes. He said, 'That's a very funny thing.'

His money and his papers were all on the right-hand side of the wallet, and he knew that yesterday there had been some on the right and some on the left. He went through the papers carefully and counted his money. Nothing was missing so far as he could remember. Then he said, 'Well, well,' because Curly's photo wasn't there any more. He went through the wallet more carefully, but it wasn't there. He put the wallet back in his pocket thoughtfully and finished the rye.

Unless someone had come in while he slept, someone other than Glorie, he knew he hadn't far to look for the photo. He wasn't going to get away as Ross any more. She, or whoever it was, must have seen his licence papers. He lit a cigarette and waited for Bugsey. He knew it would be a waste of time to try and get anything out of Glorie right now. She'd just pretend she felt bad, and that would be the end of that.

Bugsey came into the bar with a look on his face a dog gets when he thinks there's a bone around. He was wearing a stained suit of grey herringbone, and a greasy light felt hat. A red flower decorated his buttonhole. Fenner found himself wondering if it had grown there.

Bugsey wiped his mouth with the back of his hand and looked at the row of bottles with a smile of expectation. Fenner bought him a large beer and took him to the far end of the room. When they had settled, Fenner said, 'Listen, pal, how would you like to work for me?'

Bugsey's gooseberry eyes opened. 'I don't get it,' he said.

'I gotta little job you might like to handle. Nothing very much, but it's worth fifty bucks. If you an' me get along, I might put you on my pay-roll, but it'd mean kissin' goodbye to Carlos.'

'Ain't you workin' for Carlos no more?'

Fenner shook his head. 'Naw,' he said, 'I don't like his game. It stinks.'

Bugsey shook his head. 'Carlos won't like it,' he said uneasily.

'Never mind Carlos,' Fenner said. 'If I don't wantta play, I don't.'

Bugsey wagged his head. 'How do I earn fifty bucks?' he asked eagerly.

'This is a sweet job that means no work and not much worry. You remember the jane on the *Nancy W*?'

Bugsey passed his tongue over his lips. 'Am I likely to forget her?' he said. 'What a number!'

'She's upstairs in my bed, right now.'

Bugsey slopped his beer. His moonlike face showed his surprise. He said, 'In your bed?'

Fenner nodded.

'What a guy!' Bugsey was almost overwhelmed with admiration. 'I bet it cost you a heap of jack to get her in there.'

Fenner shook his head again. 'Fact was, Bugsey, I had to fight to keep her out.'

Bugsey put the beer down on the table with a click. 'You ain't kiddin'?' he said. 'You wouldn't tell a lie about a thing like that?'

'No, she's up there all right.'

Bugsey brooded, then he said in a hoarse, confidential whisper, 'You might tell me how you do it. That sort of dope comes in useful.'

Fenner thought it was time to get down to business.

'Never mind about the details, pal,' he said. 'Some guy pulled a rod on this dame and took a little meat out of her side. This guy might look in again and make a better job. I want you to sit around with a rod an' see he doesn't.'

Bugsey said in a faint, strangled voice, 'An' you're payin' fifty bucks for a job like that?'

Fenner looked startled. 'Ain't it enough?'

'That's a laugh. I'd do it for nothin'. Maybe she'd go for me.'

Fenner got up. 'Okay, come on up, I'll introduce you. Only don't go gettin' ideas. You sit outside the door, get it? A dame like that hasn't any time for hoods. That's what you said, wasn't it?'

A little crestfallen, Bugsey followed him upstairs. Fenner knocked on the door and went in. Glorie was lying in a pink satin nightdress, all ribbons and frills. She gave a little giggle when Fenner paused, staring at her.

'Isn't it a dream?' she said. 'Did you choose it yourself?'

Fenner shook his head. 'I've got a bodyguard for you. This is Bugsey. He's goin' to hang around to keep off the nasty men.'

Glorie looked Bugsey over with surprised eyes. 'He looks nasty himself,' she said. 'Come in, Bugsey, and meet a lovely lady.'

Bugsey stood in the doorway gaping.

Fenner reached forward and pulled a chair out into the passage. 'This guy's going to sit outside and work,' he said grimly. 'That's what I'm payin' him for.'

He pushed Bugsey out of the room again and nodded to her. 'I've got a little job to do, then I'll be back for a talk. Take it easy, won't you?' Then, before she could say anything, he drew the door shut. 'Get busy,' he said to Bugsey, 'and keep outta that room. No funny business. Get it?'

Bugsey shook his head. 'I couldn't start anythin' with a dame like that. Gee! She makes my head spin.'

Away from the hotel, Fenner shut himself in a telephone booth and got the Federal Building. Hosskiss came on the line after a delay. He said, 'Were you the guy who slung a bomb at one of my boats?' He sounded angry.

Fenner said, 'Never mind about that. Your boys asked for it. They're old-fashioned. This guy Carlos's got all sorts of modern ideas. He'll be usin' poison gas soon.'

Hosskiss made growling noises, but Fenner broke in, 'I want to locate a big black sedan with three C's and two sevens in the make-up of the licence plate. Can you get me that information quick?'

Hosskiss said, 'You'd better come round. There's a lot I want to talk to you about.'

Fenner glanced over his shoulder through the dirty glass of the booth into the street. 'I'm playin' the game too close,' he said. 'I ain't showin' up at your place any more. Maybe we'll fix somewhere to meet later on. What about that sedan?'

Hosskiss said, 'Hang on.'

Fenner leant against the wall of the booth and read the various scribblings on the white paintwork. When Hosskiss came over the line again, Fenner said, 'This town wants cleanin' up. The things you guys write in these booths —'

Hosskiss cut in, 'Never mind about that. I think I've found your car. Would it be Harry Thayler's bus, do you think?'

Fenner screwed up his eyes. 'Yeah,' he said, 'it could be.'

'There are others in the list, of course, but Thayler seems to be the best bet.'

'Never mind about the others. That'll do to go on with. Listen, Hosskiss, if I hand you Carlos an' his mob on a plate, will you get some work done for me?'

Hosskiss said he would.

'I want everything you can get on Thayler. I want to know all about a dame named Glorie Leadler, and as much as you can dig up about her sister, Marian Daley. Then there's Noolen; I want his history, too. You might see what you can find out about this guy Leadler, Glorie's husband. Then, when you've done all that, I want a line on a dame called Curly Robbins, who works at Nightingale's Funeral Parlour. I want to find out what Thayler knows about her, too.'

Hosskiss got quite excited. 'Hey!' he said. 'That's a job of work. Diggin' up things like that will cost money.'

Fenner sneered. 'What the hell's the use of your organization if you can't do a little thing like that? You get all that for me, an' I'll give you Carlos an' maybe I'll donate five C's to your knitting club or somethin'.'

Hosskiss said, 'Okay, I'll cover it. But it's goin' to take time.'

'Sure it'll take time. It'll mean starting from birth certificates an' working up. I want all the dope, not some of it.'

'Now listen, about this business of the bomb,' Hosskiss began heatedly, but Fenner hung up. He stepped out of the booth, wiped his hands with his handkerchief and walked in the direction of Duval Street. While he walked, his mind was busy. So Thayler was the guy who owned the sedan. That gave him ideas. There was something very phoney about the whole business. This Glorie Leadler was playing a five-ace hand. Had she any connection with Carlos? He'd caught her in one lie, why not another? Her sister had said, 'What can she want with twelve Chinese?' Why had she said that, unless Glorie had told her about the Chinese? If Glorie hadn't written the letter, and he didn't think she had, who was the writer? Obviously the letter must have been a plant to give him a key to the whole business. Therefore it followed that the writer was anxious for him to crack it open. The handwriting was a woman's. There was only one other woman at the moment in this business and that was Curly. Had Curly written the note? Or – the idea so startled him that he stopped in the middle of the street – had Marian written it herself?

A fat man bumped into him, walked round him and went on, screwing his head to scowl at him. Fenner walked on to Nightingale's.

The buzzer sounded as he opened the door. From behind the curtain Carlos suddenly appeared. The faint cloying smell of marihuana came from his clothes, and his eyes looked like pieces of glass in his white face.

Fenner was a little startled. 'Selectin' your box?' he asked pleasantly.

Carlos said, 'You want anything?'

Fenner wandered round the room. 'Oh, I look in an' have a chin with Nightingale,' he said casually. 'Good guy, when you know him. Don't see you around here much. Givin' Curly a thrill?'

Carlos leant against the counter. The atmosphere was very brittle. 'Miller says you bounced him around on the boat,' he said; 'I don't like fightin' in my mob.'

Fenner raised his eyebrows. 'No? That's too bad. Every time Miller tries to make any frill when I'm around, he's goin' to be bounced, that is if the frill doesn't like him.'

Carlos blinked. 'Reiger didn't think much of your work either,' he said.

Fenner shook his head. 'That's bad, too. But then I ain't surprised. Reiger an' I don't get on so well.'

'What with one thing and another, maybe it'd be better if you didn't work for me for a while.' Carlos studied his nails.

Fenner wandered over to him. 'Sure,' he said, 'that suits me.'

Carlos twisted his mouth. It was his idea of a smile. 'Maybe you'd like to select a box. Nice to know that you're gettin' your wishes after you're dead.'

Fenner was quite close to him now. 'Meaning that things might happen? An accident or somethin'?'

Carlos shrugged. 'You do know a lot now, don't you?' he said. 'Not that it'd help the cops. I've changed my office an' you don't know where the boat picked up or landed the Chinks, but still, you know somethin'.'

Fenner said, 'I shouldn't try it. No, I guess it'd be a dopey move to try anythin' like that.'

Carlos adjusted his tie. 'I don't care a great deal what you think,' he said, and turned away. Fenner reached out and jerked him round. 'I just want to show you where we stand, hophead,' and punched Carlos high up on his cheekbone. He didn't hit very hard, but he knocked Carlos off his feet.

Carlos lay on his back, supported by his elbows. A bruise showed on his soft white skin. He began to hiss through his teeth. He made Fenner think of some slug-like thing.

Fenner said, 'Now you know. I never let anyone talk big about my death; it makes me nervous. If you do want to start anythin' I suppose you'll have to try, but this I promise you. If you don't pull it off, I'm comin' after you. It'll take more than your mob of hoods to stop me. I'm not goin' to bother about them, it's you I'm comin' after, an' when I catch up with you I'll bend you round a pole an' break your back for you.'

Carlos got slowly to his feet. When he put his hand to his face his hand fluttered like a moth's wing.

'Dust,' Fenner said. 'Go home an' have a shot of liquor; you need it.'

Without a word Carlos went out, closing the door behind him.

Nightingale said, 'That's a hell of a thing to do.'

How long he'd been standing there Fenner didn't know. The light on his glasses hid his eyes, but Fenner could see some sweat beads on his face.

Fenner said, 'Why didn't you pick the punk up if he means all that to you?'

Nightingale showed his white, sharp teeth. 'He means nothing to me,' he said, his voice trailing off to a squeak. 'All the same, it was a hell of a –'

'Skip it,' Fenner broke in. 'It's time someone slapped that hophead down. He thinks he's the king pin in this joint.'

'He is.'

'How far in are you with him?'

Nightingale made an expressive gesture. He waved his hand round the room and shrugged. 'All this is his. I'm just his front.'

Fenner grunted. 'You keep pluggin' because you've got nothing else?'

Nightingale nodded. 'Sure,' he said; 'I gotta live.'

'Curly? Where does she come in on this?'

The weak eyes snapped behind the lenses. 'You leave her outta this.'

Fenner said, 'She's gone soft on Carlos.'

Nightingale took two little shuffling steps forward. He swung over a left that caught Fenner flush on the chin. It was meant to be a socker, but a man like Nightingale hadn't any iron in his bones. Fenner didn't even rock. He said, 'You're under my weight. Forget it.' Nightingale started another punch, then switched to his pocket. Fenner sunk his fist in his ribs. Nightingale went down on his knees with a sigh, rolled over on his side and got his gun out. Fenner stepped forward and stamped on his wrist. The gun clattered on the parquet, then bounced on to the pile carpet. Fenner knelt down and jerked Nightingale round by his coat collar.

'I said forget it.' He shook the little man. 'If you don't believe me, then you'll believe someone else some other time, but I ain't fighting with you over any dame.'

Nightingale drew his lips off his teeth, started to say something, stopped, and looked beyond Fenner, over his shoulder. His anger changed to alarm. Fenner saw a man standing behind him. He saw the miniature of the man in Nightingale's glasses. He saw an arm come up, and he tried to turn. Something exploded inside his head and he fell forward. He scraped the skin off his nose on Nightingale's coat buttons.

Chapter Four

Fenner's first reaction was to the naked light hanging in a wire basket from the ceiling. Then he noticed that the room had no windows. After that, he shut his eyes again and drifted to the steady throb inside his skull. The light burned through his eyelids, and he tried to roll over away from it. When he found he couldn't move, he raised his head and looked. The movement exploded something behind his eyes, and he had to lie still again. Then, after a while, the throb went away, and he tried again.

He found he was lying on an old mattress, and his hands were tied to the ironwork of the rusty bedstead. The room was completely bare except for the bed. The floorboards were littered with cigarette butts and tobacco ash. The dust was thick. Several pages of a scattered newspaper lay about, and the fireplace contained a pile of black ashes, as if someone had recently been burning a lot of papers. It was a nasty room, full of the smell of decay, damp and stale sweat.

Fenner rested. He made no effort to free his hands. He lay quietly, his eyes screwed up a little to avoid the rays of the light, and he breathed gently. He listened with an intentness that caught at every whispered sound. By lying like that and by listening hard, he heard sounds which at first meant nothing to him, but which he later distinguished as footsteps, the murmur of voices and the distant breaking of the rollers on the shore.

He went to sleep finally because he knew that sleep was the only thing for him at the moment. He was in no shape to try to escape. He had lost all sense of time, so when he woke he knew only that the sleep had been a good one, because he felt well again. His head ached dully, and his brain no longer rolled around inside his skull. He woke because someone was coming down the passage outside his door. He could hear the lock and the door was kicked open. He closed his eyes. He thought it was too early to take an interest in visitors.

Someone walked over to him, and the light in his eyes went away as that someone got between him and the light. There was a long silence, then a grunt and the light began to irritate him once more. Footsteps walked to the door. Fenner opened his eyes and looked. The small squat back and short legs of the man going out of the door told him nothing, but the thick oily black hair and the coffee skin made it a good guess that he was a Cuban. He went out and locked the door again.

Fenner drew a deep breath and began to work his hands. The cords holding him were tight, but not impossibly tight. He strained and pulled, chewing on his under lip as he did so. The effort made the light go black, and he had to stop. He lay still, panting a little. The only ventilation came from the transom over the door. The room was very hot and close. Fenner could feel the sweat gumming his shirt to his back. He gently wiggled his wrists. He thought, 'I've shifted them. Yes, I've done something. If I could only stop this damn headache, maybe I'd get somewhere. Now, once more.' He pulled and twisted again. His right hand, made slippery with sweat, gradually slid through the circle of cord, but he couldn't do anything about his left hand. He was caught there all right.

Slowly he sat up and felt his head with his fingers very gently. The back of his skull was tender, but there was no lump or bruise. He smiled bleakly. Then he twisted round and examined the knot that was holding his left hand. It was knotted under the bed in such a way that he could only feel it, but he couldn't see it. The knot defied all the effort he made to loosen it, and he lay back on the bed, swearing softly.

He thought, 'Only one up. I wonder who smacked me.' Carlos? He could have gone out, watched through the door and come back quietly when Nightingale was getting tough. Or was it someone else? Where was he? More important, what was going to happen to him?

He sat up on the bed again and swung his feet to the floor. Then he stood up shakily, his left hand preventing him from standing entirely upright. His head ached a lot when he stood up, but it began to pass as he moved to the door, dragging the bed with him. He satisfied himself that the door was locked, and then, pushing the bed back to the wall, he sat down again.

He'd got to get his hand free somehow, he told himself. He lay down and began to tear at the knot feverishly. His damp fingers slid off the cord, making no impression.

The sound of footfalls made him pause, and he hastily rolled on his back and slipped his wrist through the circle of cord. He'd barely done so when the door opened and Carlos came in. Reiger and Miller stood just inside the door. Carlos came over and stood by Fenner's bed. Fenner looked up and their eyes met.

Carlos said, 'Well, the punk's awake.'

Reiger and Miller came farther into the room, and Reiger shut the door. They came around the bed. Fenner looked at each man slowly. He said casually, 'What's the idea?'

Carlos was shivering a little. He was doped to his ears. Fenner could see the pin-point pupils. Carlos said, 'We're goin' to have a little talk.' He drew back his fist and hit Fenner with his small bony knuckles just below his nose. Fenner had his head moving when he saw the blow coming, but it only took a little of the steam out of the punch. He felt his teeth creak.

Carlos said, 'I owe you that one, don't I?'

Fenner said nothing. He hated Carlos with his eyes, but he knew that with his left hand pinned he wouldn't stand much chance with three of them.

Carlos said, 'So you're a private dick.' He took from his pocket Fenner's papers and scattered them over the bed. 'You certainly pulled a fast one that time.'

There was a moment's silence. Carlos sat on the bed. Fenner knew that he could nail him now. If the other two cleared off he could grab Carlos by his neck and settle with him. Maybe the other two would clear off. He'd have to wait.

Carlos leaned forward and slapped Fenner across his face. He slapped him very hard, twice. Fenner blinked his eyes, but he didn't move or say anything. Carlos sat back again. His shivering made the bed rattle against the wall. He looked a little insane. He said, 'Why have you come down here? What are you trying to find out?'

Fenner said with stiff lips: 'I told you not to try anything. Now, by God, I'm goin' to start after you. I ain't lettin' up until I've broken your lousy little back.'

Miller exploded in a high-pitched laugh. 'He's nuts,' he said, 'he's stark raving nuts.'

Carlos had to put his hands in his pockets because they trembled so much. He said, 'Listen, we're goin' to work on you. I want to know what you're doing here. Tell me quick, or I'll start on you.'

Fenner sneered. He began to pull his hand out of the cord. He did it very slowly so that they didn't notice. He said, 'Take my tip an' let me outta here.'

Carlos stood up. He motioned to Reiger. 'Work on him,' he said.

Reiger got to the bed at the same time as Fenner slipped the cord. Fenner swung his leg round in a long lightning arc. He kicked Reiger just under the knee-cap. Reiger fell down, holding his knee with both hands. His eyes opened very wide with the pain and he began to curse. Fenner sat up on the bed as Miller rushed in. Miller's hands caught his hair and jerked him over, but he swung a punch into Miller rather low down. He put a lot of steam in that punch.

Miller flopped on the floor, holding his big belly in both hands. He face glistened as he began to roll, trying to get his breath.

Carlos backed away quickly. He was scared all right. Fenner got to his feet and started after him, dragging the bed with him. Reiger caught hold of the leg of the bed and hung on. Fenner pulled, striving to get at Carlos, who in his panic had circled away from the door. The bed moved a little Fenner's way, then jerked back as Reiger hauled on it.

Carlos said in a squeaky voice, 'Get up an' fix him. Don't lie there, damn you!' He pulled a gun and pointed it at Fenner. 'Stay where you are,' he said. 'I'll blast you if you move.'

Fenner took another step forward, dragging the bed and Reiger with him. 'Go ahead,' he said. 'It's the only thing that'll save you.'

Miller climbed to his knees and came at Fenner with a rush. His great fat body knocked Fenner on to the bed. Fenner fell with his right arm under him, and for a second or so Miller could hit him as he liked. He smashed in a couple of punches that didn't do Fenner any good, then Fenner got one of his legs up and kicked him off the bed. Miller got to his feet again and Reiger came up behind Fenner and grabbed him round his throat. Miller stepped in then and slammed in three or four punches to Fenner's body. Miller was flabby, but he made his punches felt. Fenner knew he wasn't the one to get worried about, Reiger was the boy. Reiger was hugging his throat with an arm like an iron band and Fenner felt his head begin to swim. Getting his feet firmly on the floor, he stiffened his body and heaved backwards. He, the bed and Reiger all went over with a crash. Reiger let go and tried to wriggle clear.

Fenner was in a bad position. He was kneeling with his left hand twisted behind him and the bed resting on his back. The only way he could get out of the position was to heave the bed over again. As he straightened up, carrying the bed on his back, Reiger kicked out at him. Reiger's foot caught him behind his knee, and he went over. The muscles of his imprisoned arm seemed to catch fire, and, half crazy with the pain, Fenner slammed the bed over on top of Reiger. The iron headpiece caught Reiger under the chin and Fenner heaved on the bed with all his weight. Reiger's eyes started out of his head and he began to wave his arms violently. Fenner went on shoving.

Miller dropped on him and started beating him about the head, but Fenner didn't take off the pressure. He knew he'd got Reiger, and if he could stop him, he'd stand a chance with the other two. Reiger was going a blackish purple, his arms only waved feebly. Carlos ran round and jerked the bed away. Reiger flopped on his hands and knees, making a honking sound like a dog being sick.

Miller had opened a cut just above Fenner's eyes and the steady stream of blood bothered him. He groped round with his free hand. He dug his fingers into Miller's belly. Miller gave a high whinny sound and tried to get away, but Fenner hung on, heaved, bringing the bed crashing down on both of them.

Carlos stood peering down at them through the bed springs, but he couldn't get at them. He tried to pull the bed away, but Fenner held it with his arm. He kept the paralysing grip on Miller, who began to scream and thrash with his legs. He tried beating Fenner's face with his fists, but Fenner just twisted some more, kept his head on his chest, and hung on.

Carlos ran out, and Fenner could hear him shouting violently in Spanish. Miller gave a sudden heave and broke away. He went a whitish green, and flopped limply, just lay there, staring at Fenner with frightened eyes.

Fenner tried to smile, but couldn't make it. He kicked Miller away and turned the bed over slowly. He got his arm into a more natural angle. Then, working feverishly, he got the iron post out of the sockets of the bed and stood up. Even then, with his arm tied to the iron post, he was in a bad position, but not so bad as he had been. He started for the door. As he passed Reiger, who was kneeling with his back to the wall, his hand to his throat, Fenner gave him a swipe with the iron post. Reiger fell over on his side, covering his head with his arms.

Fenner took more steps and got outside the room. He felt as if he was walking through glue. His steps got slower as he reached the passage, and he suddenly fell on his hands and knees. He felt very light-headed and his chest began to hurt. He stayed on his hands and knees, wanting very badly to lie down, but he knew he had to go on. He put a hand on the wall and levered himself up again. He left a long smear of blood on the dirty yellow paper. He thought: 'Hell, I ain't goin' to make it!' and he fell down again.

There came a lot of shouting downstairs and he tried to get back in the room again. He heard men coming up the stairs fast. He thought, 'Blast this post!' and tried once more to free his hand. It seemed welded to the thing. He strugged up as two excited little Cubans came rushing at him. They all went down in a heap together. One of them grabbed him at the throat and the other tangled his legs up. These little punks were strong.

He heard Carlos's voice shout, 'Not too hard!' then something crashed on his head and he fell forward. Out of the blackness his hand encountered a face and he punched feebly, then a bright light burst before his eyes and suffocating blackness blotted out everything.

Fenner thought, 'I must have taken a beating. They think I can't start any more trouble.' He said that because he found they hadn't bothered to tie him this time. They had taken the bed away and left him in the empty room on the floor. He gave himself a little while, but when he tried to move he found he could just twitch his body.

He thought, 'What the devil's the matter with me?' He knew he wasn't tied, because he couldn't feel any cord on him, but he couldn't move. Then he became aware that the light was still on, but his eyes were so swollen that he could only see a fuzzy blur. When he shifted his head, pain like sheet lightning travelled all over him and he lay still again. Then he went to sleep.

He woke because someone was kicking him in the ribs. Not hard kicks, just heavy thumps, but the whole of his body raved at the pain.

'Wake up, punk!' Reiger said, kicking continuously. 'Not feelin' so tough now, huh?'

Fenner screwed up everything he'd got in him, rolled towards the sound of the voice, and groped with his arms. He found Reiger's legs, hugged them and pulled. Reiger gave a strangled grunt, tried to save himself, and went over backwards. He landed with a crash that shook the room. Fenner crawled towards him grimly, but Reiger kicked him away and scrambled to his feet. His face was twisted with cold rage. He leant over Fenner, beat away the upraised arms, and grabbed him by his shirt front. He pulled him off the floor and slammed him down hard.

Carlos came in and paused. 'You doin' that for fun?' he asked. There was a faint rasp in his voice.

Reiger turned. 'Listen, Pío,' he said through his teeth. 'This guy's tough, see? I'm just softening him up.'

Carlos went over and looked down at Fenner. He stirred him with his foot. Then he looked over at Reiger. 'I don't want him to croak. I want to find out things about him. I want to know why he came all the way from New York and got in with our mob. There's somethin' phoney about this, and I don't like it.'

Reiger said, 'Sure. Suppose we make this guy talk?'

Carlos looked down at Fenner. 'He ain't in shape to be roughed around just yet. We'll try him in a little while.'

They went out.

Fenner came round again a little later. There seemed to be an iron clapper banging inside his skull. When he opened his eyes, the walls of the room converged on him. Terrified, he shut his eyes, holding on to his reason.

He stayed that way for a while, then he opened his eyes again. This time the walls moved slowly and he was no longer scared. He crawled on his hands and knees across the room and tried the door handle. The door was locked. He had only one obsession now. He wasn't going to tell them anything. They had beaten him over the head so much that he had lost much of his reason, and he was no longer aware of the pain that tortured his body.

He thought, 'I've gotta get out of this. They'll go on until they kill me.' Then he remembered what they had done to the Chinese, and he went a little cold. 'I couldn't take that,' he thought. A cunning gleam came into his eyes and he put his hand on the buckle of his belt. He undid the belt and pulled it through the loops of his trousers. Then he climbed unsteadily to his feet. He had to put one hand against the wall to support himself.

With exaggerated care he threaded the long strip of leather through the buckle. Then he passed the loop over his head, drew the belt tight round his neck.

He said, 'I gotta find a nail or a hook or something. I gotta fix the other end somewhere.' He wandered round the room, searching the bare walls. He made a complete circle of the room and stopped by the door again.

He said, 'What am I going to do now?'

He stood there, his head hanging on his chest, and the belt

swinging from his neck. He went round the room again more carefully, but the walls were naked. There was no window, no hooks, only the electric light bulb high up out of his reach.

He wondered if by putting his foot through the loop made at the other end of the belt, he could strangle himself. He decided he couldn't. He sat on the floor again and tried to think. The clapper went on banging inside his skull, and he held his head in his hands, swaying to the beat.

Then he saw how he could do it. He said, 'I guess I'm not as smart as I used to be.' He crawled over to the door on his hands and knees and fastened the belt round the door handle. By lying face downwards he could hang himself all right. It'd take time, but he guessed if he stuck it he'd croak.

He spent quite a time fastening the belt securely to the handle. He made it short so that his neck was only a few inches from the brass handle, then he slid his feet away slowly until he was stretched out, his weight supported by his hands.

He had no thoughts about his finish. He could only think that he was cheating Carlos. He remained still for a few seconds, then he took his hands away, allowing his whole weight to descend on the belt. The buckle bit into his neck sharply and the leather sank into his flesh.

He thought triumphantly, 'It's going to work!' The blood began to pound in his head. The agony in his lungs nearly forced him to put his hands to the ground, but he didn't. He swayed on the belt, a blackness before his eyes. Then the handle of the door snapped off and he fell to the boards with a crash.

He lay there dazed, breathing in the hot air in great gasps. Blood trickled from his neck where the buckle had bitten into him. A sick feeling of defeat was far worse than the pain that racked his tired body.

Pulling the belt from his neck, he lay on his back staring up at the dirty ceiling. The blood from his neck set him thinking. His mind was so dazed that he couldn't piece his thoughts together, but he knew that if he kept thinking he was going to find another solution.

He stayed still for a time, then he sat up again. Once more the cunning look came into his eyes. He groped for the belt and examined the buckle. It had a sharp, short spike that caught in the belt holes. Somewhere in his arms, he knew, were his main arteries. He'd only to pierce them with the spike and he'd bleed to death.

He said, 'Nice way to go. I must be crazy not to have got round to that before.'

Laboriously he felt for the artery. When he thought he'd found it, he took the buckle and pressed the spike into his flesh.

A tiny speck of blood appeared, and he pressed harder. The artery began to pulse and throb. Then suddenly the spike sank deep and the blood welled up. He was so exhausted that he fell back on the floor. His aching head struck the wall and he went out in a bright flash of light.

A shadowy figure materialized out of the bright mist. Fenner looked and wondered vaguely if it were an angel. It wasn't, it was Curly. She bent over him and said something he couldn't hear, and he mumbled, 'Hello, baby,' softly.

The room was building up into shape and the bright mist was going away. Behind Curly stood a little man with a face like a goat. Faintly, as if he were a long way off, Fenner heard him say, 'He'll be all right now. Just make him lie there. If you want me, I'll come round.'

Fenner said, 'Give me a drink of water,' and fell asleep.

When he woke again, he felt better. The clapper in his head had stopped banging and the room stayed still. Curly was sitting on a chair near him, her eyes very heavy, as if she wanted sleep.

Fenner said, 'For God's sake –' but Curly got up hastily and arranged the sheet. 'Don't talk yet,' she said; 'you're all right. Just go to sleep.'

Fenner shut his eyes and tried to think. It wasn't any use. The bed felt fine and the pain had gone away from his body. He opened his eyes again.

Curly brought him some water. He said, 'Don't I get anything stronger'n that?'

Curly said, 'Listen, Jughead, you're sick. You're slug-nutty. So take what's given you.'

After a little while, Fenner said, 'Where am I, anyway?'

'You're in my room off White Street.'

'Please, baby, would you mind skipping the mystery an' letting me know how I got here?'

Curly said, 'It's late. You must go to sleep. I'll tell you about it tomorrow.'

Fenner raised himself on his elbows. He was ready to wince, but he didn't feel any pain. He was weak, but that was all. He said, 'I've been sleeping too long. I want to know now.'

Curly sighed. 'Okay, okay. You tough guys give me a pain.'

Fenner didn't say anything. He lay back and waited.

Curly wrinkled her forehead. 'Nightingale was mad with you. What did you do?'

Fenner looked at her, then said, 'I forget.'

Curly sniffed. 'He told me that Pío had bounced you, and taken you to his waterfront place. I wanted to know what was happening to you. Nightingale got restless when he cooled off. He reckoned he was letting Crotti down if he didn't look after you. It didn't need much persuasion from me to get him to go and find out. He comes back with you looking as if someone had been working over you. He says for me to get a croaker and to look after you.'

Fenner didn't believe it. 'That little guy took me out of Carlos's place? Didn't Carlos say anythin'?'

Curly yawned. 'He wasn't there. They were all over at the hotel.'

Fenner said, 'I see.' He lay still, thinking, then he said, 'What's the date?' When she told him, he said, 'It's still May?' She nodded. He reckoned painfully. He'd been away from Glorie for four days. It seemed a lot longer than that. Then he said, 'Carlos missed me yet?'

Curly yawned again. 'Uh-huh, but he ain't linked me or Nightingale up with it. Maybe he'll get around to it. He thinks of everything.'

Fenner shifted. He passed his fingers through his hair gently. His skull was very tender. 'That guy won't like you too much if he finds out.'

Curly shrugged. 'You're right,' she said, and yawned again. 'There's a lot of room in your bed. Would it embarrass you if I got me some sleep?'

Fenner smiled. 'You come on in.'

Curly smiled and went out of the room. She came back in a little while in a pink woolly dressing-gown. Fenner said, 'Well, that's homely, isn't it?'

She came round and sat on the far end of the bed. 'Maybe, but it's warm,' she said. She kicked off her slippers and took off her dressing-gown. 'You wouldn't think it, but I'm always cold in bed,' she said. She was wearing a pair of light wool pyjamas.

He watched her climb in beside him. 'That sleepin' suit looks kind of unromantic, too, doesn't it?' he said.

She laid her blonde head on the pillow. 'What of it?' She

yawned and blinked her eyes. 'I'm tired,' she said. 'Looking after a guy like you is hard work.'

Fenner said gently. 'Sure. You sleep. Maybe you'd like me to sing to you?'

Curly said 'Nuts,' drowsily, and fell asleep.

Fenner lay still in the darkness, listening to her deep breathing, and tried to think. He still felt dazed and his mind kept wandering. After a while he, too, went to sleep.

The morning light woke him. He opened his eyes and looked round the room, conscious that his head was clear and his body no longer ached. Although he was a little stiff as he moved in the bed, he felt quite well.

Curly sat up slowly in bed and blinked round. She said, 'Hello, how you makin' out?'

Fenner grinned at her. It was a twisted grin, but it reached his eyes all right. 'You've been a good pal to me,' he said. 'What made you do it, baby?'

She turned on her side. 'Don't worry your brains about that,' she said. 'I told you first time I met you I thought you were nice.' She closed her eyes.

Fenner said drowsily, 'What are you thinking?'

She put her hand up to his face gently. She said, 'I was just thinkin' how tough it is to run across a guy like you when it's too late.'

Fenner moved away from her. 'You mustn't look at it like that,' he said seriously.

She suddenly laughed, but her eyes were serious. 'I'll get you some breakfast. You'll find a razor in the bathroom.'

By the time he'd shaved his beard off, breakfast was on the table. He went and sat down. 'Swell,' he said, looking at the food.

The dressing-gown he'd found in the cupboard must have belonged to Nightingale. It reached to his ankles and pinched him across his shoulders.

Curly giggled at him. 'You do look a scream.'

Fenner made short work of the food, and Curly had to go outside and fry him some more eggs. She said, 'I guess you're mending fast.'

Fenner nodded. 'I'm great. Tell me, baby, does Nightingale mean anything to you?'

She poured him out some more coffee. 'He's a habit. I've been with him for a couple of years. He's kind to me, and I guess he's crazy about me.' She shrugged. 'You know how it is. I don't know anyone I like better, so I feel I may as well make him happy.'

Fenner nodded, sat back and lit a cigarette. 'What's Thayler mean to you?'

Curly's face froze. The laughter went out of her eyes. 'Once a dick, always a dick,' she said bitterly, getting to her feet. 'I ain't talking shop with you, copper.'

'So you know that?'

Curly began to stack the plates. 'We all know it.'

'Nightingale?'

'Sure.'

'But Nightingale pulled me out of that jam.'

'He owes Crotti something.' Curly took the plates away.

Fenner sat thinking. When she came back, he said, 'Don't get that way, baby. You an' I could get places.'

Curly leaned over the table. Her face was hard and suspicious. 'You're not getting anywhere with me on that line,' she said, 'so forget it.'

Fenner said, 'Sure, we'll forget it all.'

When she had shut herself in the bathroom, Nightingale came in. He stood looking at Fenner with a hard eye.

Fenner said, 'Thanks, pal. I guess you got me out of a nasty jam.'

Nightingale didn't move. He said, 'Now you're okay, you better dust. This burg's too small for you and Carlos.'

Fenner said, 'You bet it is.'

'What sort of pull you got with Crotti, policeman?' Nightingale asked. 'What's the idea?'

'Crotti has no use for Carlos. I'm gunning for that guy. This is the way Crotti wants it to go.'

Nightingale came further into the room. 'You've gotta get out of town quick,' he said. 'If Carlos knows that I've helped you, what do you think he'll do to me?'

Fenner's eyes were very intent as they watched Nightingale. 'I'm starting for Carlos. You better get yourself on the winning side.'

'Yeah. I'm on it already. You get outta here, or I'll help to run you out.' Nightingale was very serious and quiet.

Fenner knew it was no use talking to him. 'Have it your own way,' he said.

Nightingale hesitated, took a .38 special from his pocket, and put it on the table. 'That's to see you out of town safe. Crotti did a lot for me. If you're still around by tonight, you better start shooting' when you see me – get the idea?'

He went out, closing the door gently behind him.

Fenner picked up the gun and held it loosely in his hand. 'Well, well,' he said.

Curly came out of the bathroom. She saw the gun. 'Nightingale been in?'

Fenner nodded absently.

'Friendly?'

'About the same as you.'

Curly grunted. 'You ready to leave? I'm getting my car. I'll drop you anywhere.'

Fenner said, 'Sure.' He was thinking. Then he looked at her. 'Carlos is goin' to be washed up. You might like to talk now.'

Curly pursed her mouth. 'Nuts,' she said. 'Your clothes are in the cupboard. They'll do to get you to your hotel.' She went to the door. 'I'll get the bus.'

Fenner dressed as quickly as he could. His clothes looked as though they'd been mixed up in a road smash. He didn't care. When he'd finished dressing, he went to the door and stepped into the passage. His intention was to meet Curly downstairs. He walked slowly to the head of the stairs. He found that he wasn't as tough as he thought. It was an effort to move, but he kept on. At the head of the stairs he paused. Curly was lying on the landing below.

Fenner stood very still, and stared. Then he pulled the gun from his hip pocket and went down the stairs cautiously. There was no one about. When he came nearer he could see the handle of a knife sticking out of her back. He stopped and turned her. Her head fell back, but she was still breathing.

It took a great effort for him to get her upstairs. She was heavy, and he was trembling by the time he got her on the bed. He put her down gently, then snatched up the telephone. Nightingale's number was on the address pad. He dialled, standing with his eyes on Curly.

Nightingale said primly, 'This is the Funeral Parlour.'

Fenner said, 'Come over here quick. They've got Curly.' He hung up and went over to the bed.

Curly opened her eyes. When she saw Fenner she held one of her hands out to him. 'Serves me right for helping a dick,' she said faintly.

Fenner didn't dare pull the knife out. He held her so that she didn't have any weight on the handle. He said, 'You take it easy, baby; I'm gettin' help.'

Curly twisted. 'It's going to come a lot too late,' she said, then her face crumpled and she began to cry.

Fenner said, 'Was it Carlos?'

Curly didn't say anything. Blood stained her chin.

Fenner said, 'Give me a lead. Don't be a mug and let him get away with it. He'll only think you're a sucker.'

Curly said, 'It was one of his Cubans. He jumped me before I could scream.'

Fenner saw she was going very white. He said quickly: 'Why does Thayler carry your photo around with him? What's he to you?'

Curly whispered faintly, 'He's my husband.' Fenner saw she was going fast. He put his hand round her back and pulled the knife out. Her eyelids fell back and she gave a little cry. Then she said, 'That's a lot better.'

He laid her down on the bed. 'I'll even this up for you. Carlos'll pay for this,' he said.

She sneered. 'Okay, brave little man,' she whispered. 'Fix Carlos, if you like, but it won't do me any good.'

Fenner remembered seeing some Scotch, and he went over to the wall cupboard and poured out two fingers. He made her swallow it.

She gasped. 'That's right. Keep me alive until I've told you all you want to know' – bitterly.

Fenner took her hands. 'You can put a lot straight. Is Thayler in with Carlos?'

She hesitated, then moved her head a little. 'He's in it all right,' she said faintly. 'He's been a bad guy, and I don't owe him anything.'

'What's his angle?'

'Runs the labour syndicate.' She shut her eyes. Then she said, 'Don't ask me anything else, will you? I'm frightened.'

Fenner felt completely helpless. Her skin now looked like waxed paper. Only a red bubble at her lips showed that she still lived.

Someone came blundering up the stairs. Fenner ran to the door. Nightingale came in. His face was glistening. He pushed past Fenner and ran across to the bed. He was too late. Curly had died just before he came in.

Fenner stepped outside the room and pulled the door to. As he walked quickly down the passage a low wail came from behind the door. It was Nightingale.

The manager of the Haworth Hotel came round the desk quickly when he saw Fenner. 'What is all this?' he spluttered, his voice trembling with indignation. 'What do you think this joint is?'

'Don't ask me,' Fenner said, pushing past him. 'If it's a joint, where are the girls?'

The manager ran to keep up with him. 'Mr. Ross, I insist! I cannot have these disturbances!'

Fenner paused. 'What *are* you yapping about?'

'My people are afraid to go up on floor three. There's a rough hoodlum sitting up there, not letting anyone pass. I've threatened him with the police, but he says you told him to stick around. What does it mean?'

Fenner said, 'Get my check ready. I'm moving out.' He went upstairs quickly, leaving the manager protesting. There was no sign of Bugsey when he reached his room, and he kicked open the door and went in.

Glorie was sitting up in bed and Bugsey was sitting close to her. They were playing cards. Bugsey wore a pair of white shorts and his hat. Sweat was running down his fat back.

Fenner stood still. 'What's goin' on here?'

Glorie threw down her cards. 'Where have you been?' she said. 'What's happened to you?'

Fenner went in and shut the door. 'Plenty,' he said. Then, turning to Bugsey, 'What you think you're doing – a strip tease?'

Glorie said, 'He was playing for my nightie, but I beat him to it.'

Bugsey grabbed his trousers. 'You sure came in at the right moment,' he said feverishly. 'That dame's a mean card player.'

Fenner wasn't in the mood for laughter. He said, 'Get out quick and get a closed car. Park it at the rear of the building in a quarter of an hour.'

Bugsey struggled into his clothes. 'Looks like someone's been pushin' you around.'

'Never mind about me,' Fenner said coldly; 'this is urgent.'

Bugsey went out, pulling his coat on. Fenner said, 'Can you get up, do you think?'

Glorie threw the sheet off and slid to the floor. 'I only stayed in bed because it upset poor little Bugsey,' she said. 'What's been happening?'

Fenner dug himself out a new suit and changed. 'Don't stand there gaping,' he snapped. 'Get dressed. We're moving out of this joint fast.'

She began to dress. She said, 'Can't you tell me where you've been?'

Fenner was busy emptying the drawers into two grips. 'I was taken for a ride by a gang of toughs. Just shaken 'em off.'

'Where are we going?'

Fenner said evenly, 'We're goin' to stay with Noolen.'

Glorie shook her head. 'I'm not,' she said.

Fenner finished strapping the grips and stood up. He took two quick steps across the room and put his hand on her wrist. 'You're doing what I tell you,' he said.

'Not Noolen's.'

'That's what I said. I'm not standing for any comeback from you. You can walk, or I'll carry you.'

He went to the house 'phone and rang for his check. While waiting, he paced the room restlessly. Glorie sat on the bed, watching him with uneasy eyes. She said, 'What are you starting?'

Fenner looked up. 'Plenty,' he said. 'This mob started on me, and now I'm finishing it. I'm not stopping until I've bust the mystery right outta this business and got that little punk so short he'll scream murder.'

The bell-hop brought in the check and Fenner settled. Then he picked up his grips in one hand and took Glorie by her elbow with the other. 'Let's go,' he said, and together they went downstairs.

They found Bugsey sitting at the wheel of a big car. Bugsey was looking a little dazed, but he didn't say anything. Fenner climbed in behind Glorie. 'Noolen's. Fast,' he said.

Bugsey twisted round in his seat. 'Noolen's?' he said. 'Why Noolen's? Listen, you don't want to go to that guy. He's the south end of a horse.'

Fenner leaned forward. 'Noolen's,' he repeated, looking at Bugsey intently. 'If you don't like it, get out an' I'll drive.'

Bugsey gaped from Fenner to Glorie. She said, 'Go ahead, brave heart, this fella's making his orders stick.'

Bugsey said, 'Oh, well,' and drove off.

Glorie sat in the corner of the car, a sulky expression on her face. Fenner stared over Bugsey's broad shoulders at the road ahead. They drove all the way to Noolen's in silence. When they swept up the short circular drive Glorie said, 'I don't want to go in there.' She said it more in protest than in any hope of Fenner's agreeing. He swung open the door and got out.

'Come on, both of you,' he said impatiently.

It was half-past eleven o'clock as they walked into the deserted lobby of the Casino. In the main hall they found a Cuban in shirt-sleeves aimlessly pushing an electric cleaner about the floor. He looked up as they crossed towards him, and his mouth went a little slack. His eyes fastened on Glorie, who scowled at him.

'Noolen around?' Fenner said.

The Cuban pressed the thumb-switch on the cleaner and laid it down almost tenderly. 'I'll see,' he said.

Fenner made a negative sign with his head. 'You stay put,' he said shortly.

He cut across the hall in the direction of Noolen's office. The Cuban said, 'Hey!' feebly, but he stayed where he was.

Glorie and Bugsey lagged along in the rear. Fenner pushed open the door of the office and stood looking in. Noolen was sitting at his desk. He was counting a large pile of greenbacks. When he saw Fenner his face went blotchy and he swept the greenbacks into a drawer.

Fenner walked in. 'This is no hold-up,' he said shortly; 'it's a council of war.'

He turned his head and said to Glorie and Bugsey, who hung about outside, 'Come in, you two, and shut the door.'

Noolen sat very still behind his desk. When Glorie came in, he put his fingers to his collar and eased it from his neck. Glorie didn't look at him. She went over to a chair at the far end of the room and sat down. Bugsey shut the door and leaned against it. He, too, didn't look at Noolen. There was a strained tension in the room.

Noolen managed to say: 'What the hell's this?'

Fenner took one of Noolen's green dapple cigars from the desk box, clamped his teeth on it and struck a match with his thumb-nail. He spent a long minute lighting the cigar evenly, then he tossed the match away and sat on the edge of the desk.

Noolen said, 'You've got a lot of crust, Ross. I told you I wasn't interested in anything you've got to peddle. It still stands.'

Glorie said in a flat voice: 'He isn't Ross. His name is Fenner, and he's a private investigator, holding a licence.'

Fenner turned his head and looked at her, but she was adjusting her skirt, a sulky, indifferent expression on her face.

Bugsey sucked in his breath. His gooseberry eyes popped. Noolen, who was reaching for a cigar when Glorie spoke, paused. His fat white hand hovered over the box like a seagull in flight, then he sat back, folding his hands on the blotter.

Fenner said, 'If you were half alive, the news would have got round to you before.'

Noolen fidgeted with his hands. 'Get out of here,' he said thickly. 'Private dicks are poison to me.'

'You and me've got a job to do,' Fenner said, looking at the fat man with intent eyes. 'The law doesn't come into this.'

Noolen said viciously, 'Get out!'

Without any effort, Fenner hit him on the side of his jaw. Noolen jerked back; his fat thighs, pinned under the desk, saved him from going over. Fenner slid off the desk, took four quick steps away and turned a little so that he could see the three of them.

Bugsey's hand was groping in his back pocket. His face showed the indecision that was bewildering him.

Fenner said, 'Hold it. If you start somethin', I'll smack your ears for you.'

Bugsey took his hand away and transferred it to his head. He scratched his square dome violently. 'I guess I'll scram,' he said.

'You'll stay if you're wise,' Fenner said evenly. 'Carlos might be interested to know what you've been doing playin' around with a dick.'

Bugsey went a little green. 'I didn't know you were a dick,' he said sullenly.

Fenner sneered. 'Tell it to Carlos. You don't have to tell it to me.'

Bugsey hesitated, then he slumped against the wall.

Fenner glanced at Noolen, who sat in a heap, rubbing his jaw. All the fight had gone out of him. 'Okay,' he said. 'Now maybe I can get down to things. You and me are goin' to run Carlos and his mob out of town. Bugsey here can either come in on our side, or go back to Carlos. I don't care a lot what he does. If he goes back he'll have a lot of explaining. If he sticks, he'll pick up five hundred bucks a week until the job's cleaned up.'

Bugsey's eyes brightened. 'I'll stick for that amount,' he said.

Fenner felt in his wallet, took out a sheaf of notes, crumpled them into a ball, and tossed them at Bugsey. 'That's something to go on with,' he said.

Noolen watched all this in silence. Fenner came across and sat on the desk again. 'How would you like to be the king-pin in this burg?' he said. 'That's what you can be if you work with me.'

'How?' Noolen's voice was very husky.

'We'll get your little mob and me and Bugsey and we'll make the town very hot for Carlos. We'll hi-jack his boats, we'll sabotage his organization, and we'll go gunning for him.'

Noolen shook his head. 'No, we won't,' he said.

Fenner said evenly, 'You yellow big shot! Still scared?'

'I've never worked with the cops an' I never will.'

'You don't understand. Four days ago Carlos had me in his waterfront place. He made things pretty tough, but I got away. I'm making this a personal business. I'm not inviting the law to come along.'

Noolen shook his head. 'I ain't playin'.'

Fenner laughed. 'Okay, we'll make you play.'

He stood up. 'You in this?' he said to Bugsey.

Bugsey nodded. 'I'll hang around,' he said.

Fenner nodded to Glorie. 'Come on, baby,' he said. 'You, me an' Bugsey'll look after this until this punk decides to fight.'

Glorie got up. 'I don't want to play either.'

Fenner showed his teeth. 'What a shame,' he said, walking over to her and taking her arm. 'But you're not Noolen; you'll do as you're told.'

Noolen said, 'Leave her alone.'

Fenner took no notice. 'Let's go,' he said, and they went out of the room, Glorie walking stiffly beside him.

Out in the street, Fenner paused. He said to Glorie, 'We'll stay at your place.'

Glorie shook her head. 'I told you I haven't got a place.'

Fenner smiled. 'We'll go where you keep your clothes. That evening dress looks sort of out of place at this time.'

Glorie hesitated, then she said, 'Listen, I honestly don't want to be mixed up with Carlos. Will you please excuse me?'

Fenner pushed her into the car. 'It's too late, baby,' he said unpleasantly. 'I can't have anyone shootin' you up whenever they want to. You've got to stick by me for a while.'

She heaved a sigh. 'Okay. I've got a little place off Sponge Pier.'

Fenner nodded to Bugsey. 'Sponge Pier, fast,' he said.

Bugsey climbed into the car and Fenner followed him. He sat close to Glorie, keeping his grips upright between his legs. 'There's goin' to be an awful lot of run in this joint pretty soon,' he said. 'Maybe I'll get somewhere or maybe I won't, but whatever happens to me, Carlos'll go first.'

Glorie said, 'You quite hate that guy, don't you?'

Fenner looked ahead. His eyes were very cold. 'You bet,' he said curtly.

About half a mile past Sponge Pier, hidden by a thick cluster of palm trees, was a small bungalow. Bugsey ran the car through the small landscape garden and parked it outside the door. A wide piazza screened by green sun-blinds encircled the house, and every window had green wooden sun-shutters.

Fenner got out of the car and Glorie followed him. She said to Bugsey, 'The garage is at the back.'

Fenner said, 'You got a car?'

'Yes. Do you mind?'

Fenner looked at Bugsey. 'Take that rented car back. We'll use this baby's. We can't afford to be extravagant.'

Glorie said, 'Don't mind me.'

'Got a staff here?' Fenner asked, looking the house over.

'I've got a woman who runs the place.'

'That's fine. Bugsey can help her.' Once more Fenner turned to Bugsey. 'Take the car back, then come on here. Miss Leadler will tell her woman you're coming. Then you make yourself useful until I want you. Get it?'

Bugsey said, 'You're payin' the bill,' and he drove the car away.

Fenner followed Glorie into the bungalow. It was a nice place. A small Spanish woman appeared from nowhere, and Glorie waved her hand. 'This is Mr. Fenner. He'll be staying a little while. Will you fix lunch?'

The woman gave Fenner a quick look. He didn't quite like the smirk in her eyes, and she went away again.

Glorie opened a door on the left of the lobby. 'Go in there and rest yourself. I want to change.'

Fenner said, 'Sure,' and wandered into the room. It was comfortable: cushions, divans and more cushions. The open windows let out to the piazza, and the room was dim with subdued sunlight.

The Spanish woman came in and laid a table for lunch on the piazza. Fenner sat on one of the divans and smoked. He said, 'When you're through, you might get me a drink.' She took no notice of him, and he didn't bother to speak again. He sat quite still.

Glorie came in after a while. She wore a white silk dress, ankle length, and white doeskin sandals. Her red-gold hair was caught back off her ears by a red ribbon. Her mouth was very red and her eyes sparkled.

She said, 'Like me?' and pivoted slowly.

'Yeah,' he said, getting up. 'You're all right.'

She made a little grimace at him and went over to fix drinks.

The ice-cold cocktails had a bite. When they sat down to the meal, Fenner felt fine. They got through the meal without saying much. Fenner was conscious of Glorie's eyes. She kept looking at him and then, when he glanced up, she'd look hurriedly away. They talked about the bungalow and the Spanish woman and things that didn't matter.

After the woman had cleared away, Fenner lounged on the divan. Glorie moved restlessly about the room. Fenner followed her with his eyes because she was beautiful to watch. She said suddenly, 'Don't sit there doing nothing.'

'What do you want me to do?'

She went over to the window and looked out. Fenner watched her with interest.

She said, 'Come on, I'll show you my place.'

Fenner got off the divan and followed her across the lobby and into another large room. It was very bare. Polished boards, rugs and a large divan-bed, that was all. A small dressing-room and a bathroom led off to the right. She stood aside to let Fenner pass and then shut the door behind her.

He looked into the dressing-room and then into the bathroom while she waited. 'Very nice,' he said.

He could hear the sound of her breathing from where he stood. He didn't look at her. He kept moving about the room while she waited. Then he said suddenly, 'Let's talk.'

She sat limply on the bed. She put her laced fingers behind her head. Fenner looked down at her. His face was expressionless.

'Thayler's the guy who runs Carlos's labour syndicate. He

was married to Curly Robbins, Nightingale's assistant. Carlos has just killed her. You ran with Thayler. Did you know what his racket was?'

She said, 'Sit down here, and I'll talk to you.'

He sat down close to her. 'Well?'

'Give me your hand.'

He put his hand in hers. 'Did you know?' he repeated.

She gripped it hard. 'Yes, I knew,' she said.

Fenner sat very still. 'Did you know he was married to Curly?'

She lay with her eyes closed, her teeth biting her underlip. 'No.'

'You knew all about Carlos as well?'

'Yes, I knew all about him.' She sat up. She wound her arms around his neck, pulling his head down to her. Before her lips could reach his mouth he shoved her away. 'Cut it out,' he said harshly, getting to his feet. 'You don't get anywhere with me.'

He went out of the room, unlocking the door and leaving it open. He passed Bugsey wandering in from outside. He didn't say anything, but went on into the garden.

Chapter Five

Towards evening Fenner returned to the bungalow. He found Bugsey sitting on the porch steps, making patterns on the gravel path with a piece of wood. He said, as he went past, 'Still in a pipe-dream?'

Bugsey started, but before he could say anything Fenner had passed into the bungalow. He went straight to Glorie's room.

Glorie was sitting on the window-seat, dressed in a pale green wrap. She was looking out of the window, and she turned quickly as Fenner walked in. 'Beat it,' she said harshly.

Fenner shut the door. 'I've got a little story to tell you. The Federal Bureau have been digging up the past, and I've been looking the dope over. Some quite interesting stuff.'

Glorie sat on the bed. 'I'll tell you,' he said evenly. 'Some of it's just guesswork, some of it's facts, but it makes a nice little story. It starts off in a hick town in Illinois. The guy who runs this town gets himself a young wife. That's all right, but the young wife has got big ideas. She begins to spend more money than her hubby can make. The name of this guy is Leadler, and he's a politician of sorts. You married him because you thought you could get out of the cheap song-and-dance show you were touring in. Well, you did. Leadler, to keep you in silk pants, helps himself to a lot of dough that belongs to the town. You both take a powder to Florida.'

Glorie folded her hands in her lap. 'You can't do anything to me,' she said.

Fenner shook his head. 'Hell! That's not the idea,' he said. 'I wouldn't want to do anything to you. Let me go on. You and Leadler part. I don't know why, but as Thayler now appears on the scene, I take it you prefer a younger and richer man. Okay, you lose sight of Leadler, and you go for a cruise with Thayler. Before you turn up, he was married to Curly Robbins. Thayler absorbs the Chinks Carlos smuggles into the country. He pays Carlos so much a head, and sells the Chinks to sweat shops up the coast. Curly knew all about that, so it was dangerous to let her float around without being watched. Thayler gets her a job with Nightingale, who does odd jobs for Carlos. She gets good money, doesn't have to do much, and Nightingale can look after her. You want to divorce Leadler so you can marry Thayler.

Thayler never told you he was married, and you can't find Leadler. Then one day your boat comes in to Key West and you go along for an evening's fun to the local casino. You recognize Noolen as your long-lost husband. That's a surprise, isn't it?'

Glorie chewed her underlip. 'You think you're smart, don't you?' she said, stormily.

'Noolen, or Leadler, if you like, isn't doin' so well with his casino, so he's willing to give you a divorce if you pay him for it. You want the dough to give to him, but Thayler won't part. It's stalemate for a moment. You don't care a lot for Thayler, it's his dough you want. That guy certainly rolls in dough. You want to be always sure they're going to get it, and the only way you can be sure is to marry him. The cops have turned up some dirt that proves that, while you were with Thayler, you also had a Chink running around. You two kept under cover, but not well enough. This Chink used to work for Carlos. He disappeared about a couple of months ago. Maybe Thayler found out and tipped Carlos. I don't know, but he disappeared. What happened to him, baby?'

Glorie began to cry.

Fenner went on, 'Never mind. Maybe it doesn't matter. Now your mysterious sister turns up. She comes to see me. It's a funny thing, but the cops can't give me a lead on that dame. They can't dig further into your past than your song-and-dance days. This looks like your sister was a better girl than you, and she kept out of trouble. Why she came to me, and why she knew about the Chinese, Noolen and Carlos, I can't explain yet. I'll get round to it some day, but right now it's got me beat. As far as I'm concerned, its your sister who gets me to come down here. I find the situation lined up like this:

'Noolen's frightened of Thayler and Carlos. I can understand that now. He doesn't want anyone to know he's Leadler, and I bet you've told Thayler that, or if you haven't he thinks you have. You and Thayler are not getting on too well. You're quarrelling. Then, maybe, you learn that he's married, and you shoot him. You get scared and run to me. You like the look of me and you're looking round for someone to hook up with again, so after you've shot Thayler you come along to my hotel. Now you haven't killed Thayler. He's waitin' in his car parked by the boat. He nearly kills me and, later, he knows you've taken somethin' from the boat, after you shot him. Isn't that right?'

Glorie stopped crying. 'Is that all you know?' she said.

Fenner shrugged. 'It helps, doesn't it?'

Glorie didn't say anything.

'Thayler's washed up as far as you're concerned. You and I can go after him. I'm going to smash Carlos and his racket, and Thayler may as well go with him. What do you think?'

Glorie said, 'I must think. Go away now. I want to get things straight.'

Fenner got to his feet. 'I'll be waiting in the other room. Make it snappy,' he said. He went to the door and then paused. 'What was your sister to you?' he said abruptly.

Glorie shifted her eyes. 'Nothing,' she said. 'I hated her. She was mean, narrow minded and a mischief-maker.'

Fenner raised his eyebrows. 'I don't believe a lot you say,' he said, 'but maybe that's true. You're not sorrowing for her, are you?'

'Why should I?' she said fiercely. 'She got what was coming to her.'

Fenner stood by the door. Then he said slowly, 'That gives me an idea. You and Thayler were in New York at the time of her death. You two girls were almost twins. Suppose Thayler fell for her. Suppose you came in and found them, got jealous, and killed her. Suppose Thayler got those two Cubans to carve her up and get rid of her. Were those two guys workin' for him?'

Glorie said, 'Oh, run away. You'll be thinking I'm worse than I am.'

Fenner was quite startled at this new idea. He came back into the room again. 'Was that the way it went?' he said. 'Come on, did you kill Marian Daley?'

Glorie laughed in his face. 'You're nuts,' she said. 'Of course I didn't.'

Fenner scratched his head. He said, 'No, I don't think that's quite the way it went. It won't explain the guy who said she was screwy, an' it won't explain the Chink in my office. Still, it's an idea.'

He stood looking at her for several moments, then walked out of the room, leaving her polishing her nails.

Outside, Fenner went into the sitting-room. A vague feeling of excitement stirred him, a feeling that he was approaching a solution of the mystery of this business. He went over to the sideboard and helped himself to a drink.

Bugsey wandered in. 'Got one for me?' he said hopefully.

Fenner jerked his head. 'Help yourself,' he said, sitting down on the divan.

Bugsey poured a long drink and stood blinking at the glass. He took a long pull and smacked his lips.

Fenner glanced at him, but said nothing.

Bugsey fidgeted with his eyes, then said cautiously, 'She ain't nice, is she?'

'Who isn't?' Fenner was thinking about other things.

'Her – in there.' Bugsey jerked his head. 'There's somethin' the matter with her, or somethin', ain't there?'

'What is all this?' Fenner wished he'd go.

Bugsey said, 'Oh, nothing,' and finished his drink. He looked at Fenner furtively, then helped himself to another. 'Next time you go out, you might take me with you,' Bugsey said. 'Somehow I don't feel too safe alone with her.'

Fenner scowled at him. 'Listen, pal,' he said. 'Would you take a little walk? I've got a lot on my mind.'

Bugsey finished his drink. 'Sure, sure,' he said apologetically. 'I guess I'll take a little nap.' He shuffled off.

Fenner lay on the divan, holding the glass of Scotch, and staring out of the window. He stayed that way for a long time. Hosskiss, the Federal man, had been very helpful. He had turned all his information over to Fenner, and promised to try to dig up some more during the next few days. He was even hopeful of finding a line on Marian Daley, although up to now he couldn't dig up anything. Noolen, so long as he kept to Florida, was safe. He couldn't be prosecuted. Fenner wondered how smart Noolen was, and if he could be bluffed. He thought he might try and see how he got on.

He was still there when Glorie came in at sundown. She sat by his side.

Fenner said, 'Well, you thought it over?'

She said, 'Yes.'

There was a long pause. Fenner said, 'You're wondering what's goin' to happen to you, aren't you? You think if Thayler goes, you've got to start hunting around for some other man to keep you.'

Glorie's eyes hardened. 'You think of everything, don't you?' she said.

'Don't get high hat. I've thought about you, too. It's going to be tough, but there's no other way out. Thayler's on the skids, and the sooner you cut away from him the safer it's going to be for you. You don't need to worry. Take a look at a mirror. A dame like you won't starve.'

Glorie giggled. 'You're cute,' she said. 'I want to hate you, but you're too cute. Don't you ever make love to a girl?'

Fenner said, 'Let's keep to business. Never mind what I do. I'm working now, and I never play when I work.'

Glorie sighed. 'I guess that's all hooey.'

Fenner nodded. This was boring him. 'Now what about Thayler? Did you take anything from him?'

Glorie pouted. 'Why do you think I did?'

'It's a guess. Why did he want to shoot you? Revenge? Too risky. He knew you were with me. To stop you talking? Yes, that adds up.'

Glorie went over to the sideboard and opened a wooden biscuit chest. She came back with a small leather wallet. She threw it into his lap. 'I took that,' she said defiantly.

Fenner found a number of papers in the wallet. He lit a cigarette and went through them carefully. Glorie at first sat close to him, watching; then, when she saw how absorbed he was, she got up and went out on the piazza. She fidgeted around for nearly ten minutes, then she came back again. Fenner said, without looking up from his reading, 'Get a meal together, baby; I'm going to have a late night.'

She went out and left him. Later, when she came back, he was sitting where she had left him, smoking. The wallet and the papers weren't any longer in sight.

'Well?' she said.

Fenner looked at her. His eyes were hard. 'Any of those guys know you've got this place?'

She shook her head. 'No one.'

Fenner frowned. 'You don't tell me that you put this joint together all on your own?'

He wasn't sure whether her face had gone pale or whether it was a trick of the light. She said evenly, 'I wanted somewhere to go when I was sick of all this. So I saved, bought the place, and no one knows about it.'

Fenner grunted. 'You know what's in that wallet?'

'Well, I looked at it. It didn't mean anything to me.'

'No? Well, it means a hell of a lot to Thayler. There are four receipts of money paid by Carlos to him. Two IOU's from Noolen for large sums of money, and particulars of five places where they land the Chinks.'

Glorie shrugged. 'I can't cash that at the bank,' she said indifferently.

Fenner grinned. 'Well, I can,' he said, getting to his feet. 'Give me a big envelope, will you, baby?'

She pointed to a little desk in the window recess. 'Help yourself.'

He went over and put the contents of the wallet in the envelope, scrawled a note, and addressed the envelope to Miss Paula Dolan, Room 1156, Roosevelt Building, New York City.

Glorie, who had been reading over his shoulder, said, 'Who's the girl?' – suspiciously.

Fenner tapped the envelope with a long finger. 'She's the dame who runs my office.'

'Why send it to her?'

'Listen, baby, I'm playing this my way. If I liked I could turn this over to Hosskiss, the Federal man, and get him to crack down on those two guys. It would be enough for him to start an investigation. But Carlos has been tough with me, so I'm goin' to be tough with him. Maybe he'll get me before I get him, in that case the stuff gets turned over to the cops, after all. Get it?'

Glorie shrugged. 'Men are either chasing women or getting themselves into a jam because of their pride,' she said. 'I love a guy who takes on a mob single-handed to even things up. It's like the movies.'

Fenner stood up. 'Yeah?' he said. 'Who said single-handed?' He went out on to the piazza. 'I'm going to put this in the mail. I'll be right back, and then we can feed.'

On his way back from mailing the letter he passed a cable office. He paused, thought, and then went in. He wrote a cable out and took it to the desk.

The clerk checked the message and looked at Fenner hard. The message ran:

Dolan. Room 1156 Roosevelt Building, New York City. Report progress by Grosset of Daley murder. Rush. D.F.

Fenner paid, nodded, and went out again. He walked fast back to the bungalow.

Glorie was waiting for him with cocktails.

Fenner said, 'I'm in a hurry. Let's eat and drink at the same time.'

Glorie rang the bell. 'Where are you going?' she asked.

Fenner smiled. 'I'm going to see your husband,' he said gently.

'It's time he forgot his shyness and started to play ball.'

Glorie shrugged. 'A guy like that won't help you much,' she said.

While they ate, Fenner kept silent. After the meal he stood up. 'Listen, baby, this is serious. Until these guys have been washed up you've got to stay here. On no account must you leave this joint. You know too much and you've put Thayler in a spot. Any one of the mob would slit your throat if they saw you. So stay put.'

Glorie was inclined to argue, but Fenner stopped her. 'Be your age,' he said patiently. 'It won't take long, and it'll save you for some other poor sap.'

Glorie said, 'Oh, well,' and went over to the divan. Fenner walked out into the kitchen.

Bugsey had just finished supper and was making eyes at the Spanish woman, who ignored him. Fenner said, 'I'm going out. Maybe I'll be back tonight, maybe I won't.'

Bugsey lumbered to his feet. 'Shall I bring a rod?' he said.

Fenner shook his head. 'You stay here,' he said. 'Your job is to protect Miss Leadler. You keep awake and watch out. Someone might try and rub her out.'

Bugsey said, 'Aw, boss, for God's sake —'

Fenner said impatiently, 'You stay here.'

Bugsey shuffled his feet. 'That dame don't want protectin'. I'm the guy who wants protectin'.'

'What are you yapping about? You always wanted a flock of dames. She's as good as twenty dames, isn't she?' Fenner asked him, and before he could reply he left.

Noolen said, 'I thought I told you to keep outta here.'

Fenner threw two pieces of paper on the desk. 'Take a look at that,' he said.

Noolen picked up the papers, glanced at them, then stiffened. He looked sharply at Fenner, then back to the papers again.

'You'd better burn 'em,' Fenner said.

Noolen was already reaching for a match. They stood in silence until the charred ash drifted on to the floor.

Fenner said, 'That's saved you a little, hasn't it, Leadler?'

Noolen went very pale. He said hoarsely, 'Don't call me that, damn you!'

Fenner said, 'Why did Thayler lend you ten grand?'

'How did you get those?'

'Oh, I found them. I thought maybe you'd feel more disposed to play ball if you were out of Thayler's debt.'

Noolen fidgeted with his eyes. 'Glorie's been talking,' he said. There was a vicious, gritty quality in his voice.

Fenner shook his head. 'I got it from the cops. Listen, buddy, you might just as well make up your mind. If you don't play ball with me, I'll take you back to Illinois. I guess they'd be glad to see you.'

Noolen sat down. 'Sure,' he said. 'Suppose you start from the beginning.'

Fenner studied his finger-nails. 'I want a little war to start,' he said. 'First of all I want Carlos's mob jumped. I want his boats put out of action, and I want Carlos on a plate. Then we can start on Thayler.'

Noolen brooded. 'That mob's tough,' he said. 'It ain't goin' to be easy.'

Fenner grinned coolly. 'Shock tactics, buddy,' he said. 'We'll have them running in circles. Who can you get to tackle Carlos? Got any muscle-men?'

Noolen nodded. 'I know a little gang who'd do it for a consideration.'

'Okay, then it's up to you to give them what they want. I've saved you ten grand, so that's something you can spend. Why did Thayler lend you that dough?'

Noolen shifted his eyes. Fenner leant forward. 'Listen, you rat, if you don't come clean with me I'll throw you to the wolves. Hell! You're so yellow you'd want a pair of water-wings in your bath. Spill it, canary.'

Noolen pushed back his chair. 'Thayler didn't want me to divorce Glorie,' he said sullenly, 'so he lent me the dough. Lately he's been yellin' for it.'

Fenner sneered. 'You're a nice lot,' he said, getting up. 'Show me your hoods.'

Noolen said, 'I didn't say I'd do it.'

'I'm goin' to smack you in a minute if you go on like this,' Fenner said. 'Forget I'm anything to do with the cops. This burg doesn't mean anything to me. I want Carlos and his mob kicked out of here, an' I'm having the fun of seen' it done. After that I'm clearing out. It's up to you to horn in and make yourself the King Pin when they've gone.'

Noolen got up. 'I think the outfit's too big, but if that's the way you put it, I'll see how it goes.'

They went out together. A four-minute drive brought them to a pool room on Duval Street. Noolen walked in, followed by Fenner. The barman nodded to Noolen, who went on through the back.

In a large room with one billiard-table and two green-shaded lamps, five men stood around making the atmosphere thick with tobacco smoke.

They all looked up quickly as Noolen and Fenner walked in. One of them put his cue in the rack and slouched out of the room.

Noolen said, 'I wantta talk to you boys.'

They came drifting up through the smoke, their faces expressionless and their cold eyes restless. Noolen jerked his thumb at Fenner. 'This guy's Fenner. He's been gettin' ideas about Carlos's mob. Thinks it's time we rode them outta town.'

They all looked at Fenner. Then a tall thin man, with a cut-away chin and watery, vicious eyes said, 'Yeah? Well, that's a swell idea. That'll get us all a bang-up funeral, sure thing.'

Fenner said quietly, 'Let me know these guys.'

Noolen said, 'That's Schaife,' indicating the man who had just spoken. 'Scalfoni in the green shirt, Kemerinski holdin' the cue, and Mick Alex the guy with the squint.'

Fenner thought they were a fine collection of rats. He nodded. 'Let's get together,' he said, wandering over to the long padded seats, raised to overlook the billiard-table. 'How about some drinks?'

Schaife said to Noolen, 'Who's the guy, boss?'

Noolen smiled sourly, 'He's the orignial white-headed boy,' he said. 'You won't go wrong with him.'

They all sat down on the bench and fidgeted until the barman brought drinks. Fenner said, 'This is my party. Noolen's the guy who'll pay for it.'

Scalfoni, a little dried-up Italian, said, 'I gotta date with a dame in a little while. Suppose we get down to things.'

The others grunted.

Fenner said, 'Carlos has been the big shot in this town too long. We're going to make things so hot for him he's going to take a powder. I want you boys to get together on this. This ain't a picnic, it's war.'

'What's it worth?' Schaife said.

Fenner glanced at Noolen. 'That's your side of it.'

Noolen thought, then he said, 'Two grand each and a safe job when I'm in the saddle.'

Kemerinski picked his nose thoughtfully. 'You goin' to run Carlos's racket?' he said to Noolen.

Noolen shook his head. 'I've got a racket that's a lot better than that. You leave all that to me.'

Kemerinski looked at Schaife. 'Two grand ain't an awful lot, but I'd like to smack that mob if I could get away with it.'

Schaife said, 'Make it three.'

Noolen shook his head. 'Can't do,' he said briefly. 'Two's ample.'

There was a moment's silence, then the squint-eyed Alex said, 'That's okay with me.' The others hesitated, then agreed. Fenner blew out his cheeks. 'So far so good,' he thought.

'We shall want a boat,' he said. 'Any of you guys got a motor-boat?'

Kemerinski said he had.

Fenner nodded. 'There's a spot just north of Key Largo, called where Thayler makes the exchange and takes the Chinks for the Black Cæsar's Rock. That's where Carlos keeps his boats. That's rest of the ride. I guess we might go out an' look that burg over.'

Scalfoni swung his short legs. 'I got just the thing for those guys,' he said, with a cold grin. 'How would you like to take a load of bombs with you?'

Fenner looked vaguely round the room. 'Bombs?' he said. 'Sure, bring bombs.' A fixed ice-cold look crept into his eyes. 'Sure,' he repeated, 'that's quite an idea.'

Noolen said uneasily, 'The cops'll make a hell of a row about bombs.'

Fenner shook his head. 'The cops won't worry about Carlos. They'll hang out bunting when that guy croaks.'

Scalfoni got up. 'When do we go?' he said. There was a tight eagerness in his voice.

'We'll go now. We'll go just as soon as the boat's ready an' you boys have collected some artillery.'

Scalfoni hesitated, then shrugged. 'I gotta date, but I guess she'll have to wait. This sounds like it's goin' to be quite a party.'

Fenner said, 'Where's your boat?' – to Kemerinski.

'It's in the harbour opposite the San Francisco Hotel.'

'Okay. Suppose you boys meet me in an hour's time on the boat?'

They all said they'd do that, and Fenner went out with

Noolen. He said gently, as they got into the street, 'If I were you, I'd go along to the cops and get protection. If Carlos thinks you're in this he might get tough with the Casino. You keep out of sight until it's over. Tell the cops you want some officer over at your place, that you're expecting trouble.'

Noolen looked uneasy, and said he'd do that, and went off into the darkness.

Keeping to the back streets, Fenner headed for the waterfront. He walked fast, his hat pulled well down over his face, and his eyes searching the black shadows as he went along. He had no intention of running into any of Carlos's mob just at present. He knew Carlos must be looking for him. Fenner told himself the next twenty-four hours ought to be a lot more interesting than the last twenty-four hours.

As he approached the waterfront through Negro Beach he saw ahead of him a car drawn up under a lamp standard, with parkers on. He looked hard at the car and came on, slowing his pace and not quite knowing why he did so. Somehow, in the almost deserted dark street that car looked too isolated, too obviously loitering. He suddenly ducked into a doorway because he noticed the curtain of the rear window had shifted. There was no wind, and he had an uncomfortable feeling that someone had been watching him come down the street.

The sound of an engine starting came to him in the silence, and gears grated, then the car began to move forward slowly. Fenner stood in the doorway until the red tail-light disappeared round the bend in the road. He rubbed his chin thoughtfully, then stepped out on to the pavement again.

He didn't go forward, but stood very still, listening. Faintly he could hear the whine of a car, and a cold little smile hit his mouth. The car had gone forward only to turn. It was coming back.

He ran across the road fast and stepped into another doorway in the dark shadows. Squeezing himself against the brickwork, he felt for his gun and jerked it from his shoulder holster. He thumbed back the safety-catch and held the gun, with its blunt nose to the star-filled sky.

The car swung round the bend. It was gathering speed. Its only lights were its parkers, and as it swept past a blaze of gunfire spurted from the side window.

Fenner could hear the patter of bullets thudding against the wall on the opposite side of the road, where he had been. Some-

118

one was grinding a Thompson, and Fenner couldn't help being thankful that he had crossed the road. He fired three times at the car as it went past him. He heard the crash of the glass as the windshield went, and the car lurched across the road and thudded up the kerb, then smashed into a shop window.

Running from his doorway, Fenner went a little way up the street, passing the car, and ducked down a dark alley. He went down on one knee and peered round, watching.

Three men darted out of the car. One, he thought, was Reiger. They ran for cover. Fenner got the middle man in his gun-sight and squeezed the trigger. The man staggered, tried to keep his balance, then fell on his face in the road. By that time the other two had darted into doorways. They began firing at the mouth of the alley, one with an automatic and the other with a Thompson. Fenner didn't bother about the man with the automatic, but the Thompson bothered him a lot. The bullets chipped away the brickwork of the wall, and he had to crawl away from the opening as splinters of concrete made things dangerous.

Remembering the night on the boat, Fenner crawled further away. He wasn't risking having a bomb tossed at him.

Someone called, 'You better duck in here.'

He saw a door on his left open and a figure standing in the doorway. 'Shut that door and get under cover,' he shouted. 'Look lively.'

It was a woman who spoke. She said unemotionally, 'Shall I ring for the cops?'

Fenner slid over to her. 'Beat it, sister,' he said. 'This is a private row. You stay indoors; you're likely to get hurt standing there.' Just as he finished speaking a blinding flash and a violent explosion came in the mouth of the alley. A sudden rush of wind flung Fenner forward and he and the woman went over with a crash into the narrow passage of the house.

Fenner rolled over and kicked the front door shut. He said 'Wow! These guys've got bombs.'

The woman said with a quaver in her voice, 'This joint won't stand another like that. It'll fall down.'

Fenner got unsteadily to his feet. 'Let me into a front room,' he said quickly. He moved in the darkness where he thought a room ought to be, and stumbled over the woman, who was still sitting on the floor. She wound her arms round his legs and held him. 'Forget it,' she said shortly. 'You start firing from my window and they'll throw another bomb at you.'

Fenner said, 'Then let me out of here' – savagely.

Faintly the sound of a siren coming fast reached his ears.

The woman said, 'The cops!' She let go of Fenner and got to her feet. 'Got a match?'

Fenner made a light and she took the spluttering flame from his fingers. She went over to a naked gas-burner and lit it with a plop. She was a short, fat, middle-aged woman with a square chin and determined eyes.

Fenner said, 'I guess you did me a good turn. If I'd been outside when that pineapple went off, I should have been sticking to the wall. Now, I guess I better beat it before the cops start having a look round.'

The siren came up with a scream and died away in a flurry as brakes made tyres bite into the road. She said, 'You better stay here. It's too late to go out now.'

Fenner hesitated, checked his watch, found he had still some forty minutes before meeting the mob, and nodded. 'Somehow,' he said, 'you remind me of my best girl. She was always getting me out of a jam.'

The woman shook her head. A little gleam of humour showed in her eyes. 'Yeah?' she said. 'You remind me of my old man when he was around your age. He was quick and strong and tough. He was a good man.'

Fenner made noises.

She went on. 'Go down the passage and sit in the kitchen. The cops'll come in a minute. I know the cops around here. I'll fix 'em.'

Fenner said, 'Okay,' and he went into the kitchen and lit the big paraffin lamp. He shut the door and sat in a rocking-chair. The room was poor, but it was clean. The mat on the floor was thin and threadbare. There were three religious prints on the wall and two big turtle shells each side of the fireplace. He heard a lot of talking going on, but he didn't hear what was being said. To hear, he would have to open the door, and he thought they might see the light. So he just rocked himself gently and thought about Reiger. That mob was tough all right. His head still swam with the force of the explosion. Then he felt inside his coat, took out his wallet and peeled off five ten-dollar bills. He got up and put the bills under a plate on the dresser. Somehow he thought the woman wouldn't like to take money from him, and from the look of the room she needed it.

After a few minutes she came in. She nodded to him. 'They've gone,' she said.

Fenner got out of the chair. 'That's mighty nice of you. Now I guess I'll run away.'

She said, 'Wait a minute, stranger. Was that Carlos's mob?'

Fenner looked at her thoughtfully. 'What do you know about that mob?' he asked.

Her eyes grew hard. 'Plenty. If it weren't for those punks, my Tim would be here now.'

Fenner said, 'Yeah, it was them all right. What happened to Tim?'

She stood still, a massive figure of granite solidness. 'Tim was a good guy,' she said, looking straight at Fenner. 'He wasn't rich, but he got by. He had a boat and he took parties out in the gulf fishin'. Then this Carlos wanted him to take Chinks in the boat. He offered to pay, but Tim wasn't playing. He was like that. He was strong and tough, and he told Carlos no.

'Carlos couldn't get his own way, so he kills my man. Well, it ain't what happens to the one who gets killed. It's what happens to the one who gets left. Tim died quick; went out like a light. But I don't forget quick. I guess in time I'll go dead inside and I'll find things working out easier than they are now, but right now I'd like to do things to that Carlos.'

Fenner got to his feet. He said gently, 'Take it easy. Carlos'll pay for that, all right. It wouldn't get you anywhere if you did kill him. Leave Carlos to me. I gotta date with him.'

The woman said nothing. She suddenly stuffed her apron in her mouth and her face crumpled. She waved Fenner to the door wildly, and as he went out she sank on her knees by the rocking-chair.

When Fenner got down to the harbour, Schaife was waiting for him outside the San Francisco Hotel. They went in and had two quick drinks and then Fenner followed him down to the waterfront.

Schaife said, 'I've got two Thompsons and a lotta shells. Salfoni's brought a bag of bombs. God knows if those bombs are any use. He makes 'em himself. That guy's been itchin' to throw them at someone ever since he got the idea.'

Fenner said, 'He'll get his chance tonight.'

Kemerinski's boat was of a good size. Alex and Scalfoni were smoking, waiting. Fenner stepped aboard as Kemerinski appeared from the engine cockpit. He grinned at Fenner. 'Everything okay,' he said. 'We can go when you say so.'

Fenner said, 'Sure. We've got nothing to wait for. Let her go.'

The other three got on board, and Kemerinski went below and started the engine. The boat began to throb and Schaife shoved her nose off from the harbour wall.

Fenner said, 'We'll land on the village side and walk over. Maybe we'll have to leave in a hurry.'

Kemerinski grunted. 'This old tub ain't too fast,' he said, nosing the boat carefully through the lights towards the open gulf.

Scalfoni came up and climbed into the cockpit. His greasy skin shone in the dim light. 'I got the bombs,' he said. 'Gee! I'm sure goin' to get a kick when they go bang.'

Fenner took off his hat and scratched his head. 'These other guys've got bombs, too,' he said. 'They threw one at me about an hour ago.'

Scalfoni's jaw dropped. 'Did it go off?' he asked.

Fenner looked at him and nodded. 'Sure, it wrecked a house. I'm hoping you've made a good job with your home-made bangs. We might need them.'

Scalfoni said, 'Jeeze!' and went away to have another look at his bag.

It didn't take much longer than fifteen minutes before Fenner spotted distant lights. He pointed them out to Kemerinski, who nodded and said, 'Black Cæsar.'

Fenner stretched and climbed out of the cockpit. He walked over to the other three who were sitting on the foredeck, watching the lights. 'Let's get this right,' he said. 'We've come here to put Carlos's boats out of action. We've got to do this quick and with the least trouble. Scalfoni, you carry the bombs. Schaife and me will have the Thompsons, and Alex will cover us with his rod. Kemerinski will stay with the boat. Okay?'

They grunted.

As the boat ran into the small natural harbour, Schaife unslung the two Thompsons and passed one to Fenner. Scalfoni came up from the cabin, a black bag in his hand. 'Don't you guys crowd me,' he said. 'These pineapples are touchy things.'

They all laughed.

Alex said, 'Some guy'll put a slug in that bag, sure thing. It'll save you a burial, anyway.'

The boat swept in a half-circle, and came up to the side of the harbour wall as Kemerinski reached forward and cut the switch. The engine died with a little flurry.

Schaife, standing in the stern, jumped on to the wall and Alex tossed him the bowline. He held the boat steady until the others landed. Kemerinski handed up the bag of bombs tenderly to Scalfoni.

Fenner said, 'Watch out. Soon as you hear the bombs, get the engine started. We might have to leave in a hurry.'

Kemerinski said, 'Sure, that'll be okay. Watch yourselves, you guys.'

They moved towards the village. The road leading from the harbour was rough and narrow. Big stones lay about, and once Scalfoni tripped. The others swore at him uneasily. 'Careful, you punk,' Alex said; 'watch how you walk.'

Scalfoni said, 'I'm watchin' okay. The way you're goin' on, you'd think these pills were dangerous. Maybe they won't go off at all.'

Fenner said, 'We'll take the back streets. Two of you go first, and Scalfoni and I'll follow you. We don't want to attract attention.'

It was a hot night with a bright moon. Both Fenner and Schaife carried the Thompsons wrapped in a piece of sacking. They skirted the village and crossed the island through a series of small squares and dark alleys. The few fishermen they did meet glanced at them curiously, but could make out nothing except shadowy outlines.

After a steep climb they suddenly came to the sea again, sparkling several hundred feet below them.

Fenner said, 'I guess this is it.'

Down the steep incline they could see a large wooden cabin, a long concrete jetty, and six big motor-boats moored morings set in the reinforced wall. Two lights gleamed through two windows of the cabin, and the door stood half open, sending a strip of light on the oily water.

They stood silently looking down. Fenner said, 'Get the bombs out. Each of you take a couple. Scalfoni has the rest. We'll attack the cabin first. When it looks safe enough tackle the boats. They're all to be sunk.'

Scalfoni opened the bag and took out two bombs. He handed them to Fenner. The bombs were made of short sections of two-inch pipe. Fenner stood waiting until Scalfoni had given each man a couple of the stuffed pipes, then he said, 'Schaife and I will look after the cabin. You, Scalfoni, get down to the boats. Alex, stay here and come down if we get into trouble.'

Scalfoni opened his shirt and piled bombs inside.

'You have a fall now, an' you'll certainly be in a mess,' Fenner said, with a little grin.

Scalfoni nodded. 'Yeah,' he said, 'it makes me nervous to breathe.'

Fenner held the two bombs in his left hand and the Thompson in his right. 'Okay,' he said, 'let's go.'

Moving slowly, Schaife and Fenner began to slide down the incline. Fenner said, 'You go to the right and I'll take the left. I don't want any shootin' unless it's necessary.'

Schaife's thin face sneered. 'It'll be necessary all right,' he said.

Halfway down they both paused. A man had come out of the cabin and he walked along the wall.

Fenner said, 'That complicates things.'

The man stood on the wall, looking out to sea. Fenner began sliding down again. 'Stay where you are for a bit,' he said softly to Schaife. 'He might hear two of us.'

Down Fenner went silently. The man stood, his back turned, motionless. Fenner reached the waterfront and stood up. He put the two bombs inside his shirt. He was so conscious of the man that he didn't shrink at the coldness of the metal against his skin. Holding the Thompson at the ready, he walked softly down the wall. When he was thirty feet from the man, his foot touched a small stone which rolled into the water, making a loud splash. Fenner froze. Standing quite still, his finger curled round the trigger.

The man glanced over his shoulder, saw Fenner and jerked round. Fenner said, 'Hold the pose,' jerking up the Thompson.

In the moonlight Fenner could see that the man was a Cuban. He could see the whites of his eyes as they bolted out of his head. The Cuban shivered a little with shock, then he dropped on his knees, his hand going inside his coat. Fenner swore at him softly and squeezed on the trigger. He gave him a very short burst from the gun. The Cuban fell back, his hands clutching at his chest; then he rolled over into the water.

Fenner moved fast. Two big drums of petrol stood close by and he ducked behind them. He got there a split second before a machine-gun opened up from the cabin. He heard the slugs rattle on the drum, and a strong smell of petrol told him the drum was pierced.

The machine-gun kept grinding and there was such a hail of bullets that Fenner had to lie flat, his face pressed into the sand, expecting any second to feel the ripping slugs tear into his body. He put his hand in his pocket and took out the two bombs. He balanced one of them in his hand, then tossed it over the drum in the direction of the cabin. He heard it strike something and then drop to the ground.

He thought, 'So much for Scalfoni's home brew.'

The machine-gun had stopped, and the silence that followed its vicious clatter was almost painful. He edged his way to the side of the drum and peered round cautiously. The lights of the cabin had been put out and the door had been shut. He groped for the other bomb, found it, and threw it at the door. Even as his hand came up the machine-gun spluttered into life, and he ducked back just in time.

The bomb hit the door and a sheet of flame lit up the darkness, followed by a deafening noise. Brick splinters and wood whizzed overhead, and the force of the concussion made Fenner's head reel. He revised his opinion of Scalfoni's bombs after that. The machine-gun stopped. Again looking round the drum, Fenner saw that the door had been ripped so that it hung from one hinge. The woodwork and paint was smoke-blackened and splintered. Even as he looked, two more violent explosions occurred from the back of the cabin. He guessed Schaife was doping his stuff.

Resting the Thompson on the top of the drum, he fired a long burst into the cabin and ducked down again. Someone replied from the wrecked cabin with a straggly burst from the machine-gun and then Fenner gave him half the drum. After that there was a long lull.

Glancing up, Fenner could just make out Scalfoni crawling down the slope, clutching his chest with one hand. He looked very much exposed as he moved on down, but Fenner could imagine his triumphant grin. He must have been spotted coming down, because someone started firing at him with an automatic rifle. Scalfoni didn't lose his head. He put his hand inside his shirt, pulled out a bomb, and heaved it at the cabin. Fenner followed the bomb in flight, then flattened himself in the sand. He had a horrible feeling that the bomb would fall on his head.

The bomb struck the cabin and exploded with a tearing, ripping noise. A long flash lit up the sky and then the roof of the cabin caught on fire. Scalfoni came down fast without drawing any more shooting. Bent double, he ran past the cabin and joined Fenner behind the drum.

'Jeeze!' he said excitedly ... 'They work! What a night! What a night! I wouldn't've missed this for all the janes in the world.'

Fenner said, 'Watch out! They'll be coming out.'

Scalfoni said, 'Lemme give 'em just one more. Just one more to make up their mind for them.'

Fenner said, 'Sure, enjoy yourself.'

Scalfoni slung the bomb into the open doorway. The explosion that followed was so violent that although they were crouching down behind the drum they both suffered a little from the concussion.

A moment later someone screamed, 'I'm done. I'm comin' out. Don't do any more – don't do any more.'

Fenner didn't move. 'Come on out, with your mitts high.'

A man came staggering out of the blazing cabin. His face and hands were cut with flying glass, and his clothes were almost all torn off. He stood swaying in the flickering light of the flames, and Fenner saw that it was Miller. He came out from behind the drum, his lips just off his teeth.

Schaife came running up, his thin face alight with excitement. 'Any more of them?' he asked.

Miller said, 'The others are dead – don't touch me, mister.'

Fenner reached out and grabbed him by his tattered shirt. 'I thought I settled your little hash a while back,' he said unpleasantly.

Miller gave at the knees when he recognized Fenner. 'Don't start on me!' he blubbered.

Fenner cuffed him with his free hand. 'Who else is in there?' he said. 'Come on, canary, sing!'

Miller stood trembling and shuddering. 'There ain't any more,' he whined. 'They're all dead.'

Alex came running up. Fenner said to him, 'Take care of this guy. Treat him nicely. He's had a nasty shock.'

Alex said, 'Yeah?' swung his fist and knocked Miller down, then he booted him hard.

Fenner said, 'Hey! Don't get too tough. I want to talk with that punk.'

Alex said, 'That's all right. I'll have him in the right frame of mind.' He went on booting Miller.

Fenner left them and went down the wall towards the boats. Scalfoni was waiting for orders.

Fenner said, 'Scuttle 'em. Keep one. We'll go round the island an' pick Kemerinski up. It'll save walkin'.'

He went back to Miller, who had dragged himself off the ground and was imploring Alex to let him alone. Fenner told Alex to go and help Scalfoni. Fenner said to Miller, 'I told your little louse what would happen. This is only the start of it. 'Where's Thayler?' he repeated. 'Talk, you punk, or I'll spread your insides.'

Miller said, 'He don't come here. Honest, I don't know where he is.'

Fenner showed his teeth. 'We'll see about that,' he said.

Scalfoni came running up. 'They're fillin',' he said. 'Suppose I toss in a few bombs to make sure.'

Fenner said, 'Why not?'

A few minutes later the shattering roar of the bombs exploding filled the silent harbour, and clouds of dense black smoke drifted from the boats.

Fenner said to Miller, 'Come on, punk, you're going for a ride.' He had to shove Miller in front of him at the end of the Thompson. Miller was so terrified that he could hardly walk. He kept on mumbling, 'Don't give it to me. I want to live, mister, I want to live.'

The others were already in the boat waiting for them.

When they got on board, Schaife started the engine. 'Gee!' he said. 'This is the grandest night's work I've ever done. I never thought we'd get away with it.'

Fenner groped for a cigarette and lit it. 'The fun'll start as soon as Carlos hears about it,' he remarked. 'I said shock tactics would succeed, and they have. Now Carlos knows what he's up against, the rest isn't going to be so easy.'

They ran the boat round the island and signalled to Kemerinski, who started up his boat and joined them outside the harbour. They all got into Kemerinski's boat, Alex dragging Miller along with him. Scalfoni was the last to leave and before he did so, he opened the cocks and scuttled the boat.

As he climbed on board Kemerinski's boat he said, 'I guess it's tough sinkin' these boats. I could have done with one of them myself.'

Fenner said, 'I thought of that, but Carlos still has a fair-size gang, an' he'd have got them back. This is the only way.'

As Kemerinski headed the boat out to sea he wanted to know what had happened. 'I heard the uproar,' he said excitedly. 'It certainly got the village steamed up. They guessed what was gon' on, and no one had the guts to go an' watch the fun.'

Fenner said to Alex, 'Bring the punk into the cabin. I want to talk to him.'

Alex said, 'Sure,' and brought Miller down into the small brightly lit cabin.

Miller stood shivering, staring at Fenner with bloodshot eyes.

Fenner said, 'Here's your chance, canary. You talk and you'll survive. Where can I find Thayler?'

Miller shook his head. 'I don't know,' he mumbled. 'I swear I don't know.'

Fenner looked at Alex. 'He don't know,' he said.

Alex swung his fist hard into Miller's face. There was the faint sound of his arm in flight, then a thud as his fist crushed Miller's face.

Fenner repeated coldly, 'Where's Thayler?'

Miller sobbed, and mumbled something. Fenner said, 'Okay, leave him to me.' He reached inside his coat and pulled out his gun. He walked over to Miller and bent over him. 'Get up,' he said harshly. 'I'm not making a mess inside here. Come on up on deck.'

Miller looked into the gun barrel, his eyes bulging, then he said in a low, even voice, exhausted with terror, 'He's over at the Leadler dame's joint.'

Fenner remained squatting. He was very still. 'How did he know about it?' he said at last.

Miller leaned his head against the wall. Blood continued to drip from his nose and his eyes never left the gun. 'Bugsey phoned him,' he whispered.

'Bugsey?'

'Yeah.'

Fenner drew a deep breath. 'How do you know this?'

With Miller, fear had worn itself out, leaving him with the calmness of death. He said as if he was very tired, 'I was just goin' over when you arrived. Thayler 'phoned me. He said Bugsey had got him on the 'phone and told him where the Leadler dame was hiding. Thayler said for me to come, and he was gettin' Nightingale, too.'

Fenner straightened and ran to the cabin door. He shouted to Kemerinski, 'Push your tub. We've got to get back fast.'

Kemerinski said, 'She can't do any more. She'll bust.'

'Then bust her,' Fenner said. 'I want more speed.'

When the boat slid into Key West harbour Fenner said, 'Alex, you take this Miller to Noolen. Tell him to hide him until I give the word, then I'll hand him over to the cops.'

Alex said, 'Hell! Suppose we bump him an' shove him into the drink?'

Fenner's eyes snapped. 'Do what I say.'

Schaife was already making the boat fast. They all crowded off the boat. Then Fenner saw the sedan parked in the shadow. He yelled, 'Get down – look out!' and flung himself flat.

Out of the wide window of the car came gunfire. Fenner had his gun out and fired three times. The others had fallen flat except Miller who was apparently too dazed to do anything. A stream of bullets from the sedan cut across his chest and he crumpled up soundlessly.

Scalfoni suddenly got to his feet, ran a little way towards the car and tossed his last bomb. Even as the bomb left his hand he clawed at his throat and went over solidly. The bomb, falling short, exploded violently and rocked the car over on its side.

Fenner scrambled to his feet, yelling like a madman and rushed across the street, firing from his hip. Three men crawled out of the car. One of them fumbled with a Thompson. They all seemed dazed with the concussion. Fenner fired at the man with the Thompson, who pitched forward on his face. Schaife came blundering up, charged one of the remaining men, and went over with him, hammering at his head with his gun butt.

The remaining man twisted aside and fired point blank at Fenner, who hardly noticed the streak of blood that appeared suddenly in the middle of his right cheek. He kicked the man's legs from under him, stamped on his wrist so that his gun fell from his hand, and then leaned over him, clubbing him senseless with his gun butt. As he straightened up another car came round the corner and charged down. Out of it, gunfire.

Fenner thought, 'This is the bunk.' He zigzagged behind the overturned sedan. Bullets chipped the street at his feet. Schaife, trying to get under cover, gave a croaking yell and began to walk in circles. More gunfire from the car, and down he went.

From behind the sedan Fenner fired four shots at the other car, then he glanced round to see who was left. Alex and Kemerinski had got back to the boat. Even as he looked, Kemerinski opened up with the Thompson. The night was suddenly alive with gunflashes and noise.

Fenner thought that it was time he got moving. Alex and Kemerinski in their position could take care of any number of hoods. He wanted to get to the bungalow. He waited his opportunity, then, keeping the overturned car between him and the line of fire, he backed away quickly and ducked down the nearest alley.

In the distance he could hear the sound of police whistles, and he dodged down another alley away from the approaching sound. He was too busy to risk getting hauled in by the cops.

A taxi crawled past the alleyway as he emerged into the main street. Running forward, Fenner signalled the driver, who crowded on brakes. Fenner jerked open the door, giving the driver the bungalow address. 'Make it fast, buddy,' he said. 'I mean fast.'

The driver engaged his gears and the taxi shot away. 'What's breaking around here?' he asked, keeping his eyes on the road. 'Sounds like a battle going on.'

'Sure,' Fenner said, leaning back, 'battle's the right word.'

The driver leaned his head out of the cab and spat out. 'I'm glad I'm going the other way. It sounds kind of dangerous around here.'

Fenner didn't let the driver take him right to the bungalow. He got him to stop at the corner of the road, then he ran fast down towards the bungalow. Lights were showing in the front rooms, and as he walked up the short circular drive he saw someone come away from the front door. He put his hand inside his coat and loosened his gun from its shoulder holster.

A boy with a peaked cap paused at the sound of Fenner's approach, and then came towards him. He was a messenger. He said, 'You ain't Mr. D. Fenner?'

Fenner said, 'Sure. Got a telegram for me?'

The boy gave him an envelope and his book. While Fenner scratched his initials, the boy said, 'Been ringin' for quite a while. The lights are on, but no one's at home.'

Fenner gave him a quarter. 'That's how we fool burglars, son,' he said, and went on up to the house. He shoved the cable into his pocket and tried the front door, opened it, and stepped inside.

In the front sitting-room Bugsey lay on the carpet, a small pool of blackish blood making a circle round his head. His gooseberry eyes were half shut and stared sightlessly at Fenner. His mouth puckered, showing his yellow teeth in a frightened, whimpering snarl.

Fenner stood looking. He could do nothing. Bugsey was dead all right. Fenner pulled his gun out and walked slowly into the hall. He stood listening, then he went into the bedroom. Thayler sat in the small tub chair, a look of startled surprise on his face. A little congealed blood traced its way from his mouth to his shirt-front. His eyes were blank and fixed.

Fenner said aloud, 'Well, well,' and then he looked round the room. It was easy to see what had happened. Thayler had been sitting facing the door. Possibly he'd been talking to Glorie. Then someone Thayler knew walked in. Thayler must have looked up, seen who it was, not taken fright, and then that someone had shot him through his chest.

Fenner went over to him and touched his hand. It was growing cold, but there was still a little warmth in it.

A chair grated as if someone had eased it back. The sound came from the kitchen. Fenner stood very still, listening. The chair grated again. Fenner stepped to the door and peered out. Then, moving very silently, he entered the kitchen, holding his gun forward.

Nightingale stood holding on to the back of a kitchen chair. He held a blunt-nose automatic in his hand, but when he recognized Fenner his hand dropped limply to his side.

Fenner said, 'Hurt?' There was something about the way Nightingale was holding himself that made him ask the question.

'I got 'em all in my belly,' Nightingale said slowly. He began to work his way round the chair, and when Fenner came over to help him he said a little feverishly, 'Don't touch me.' Fenner stood back and watched him manoeuvre himself down into the chair. When he finally sat, sweat ran down his face.

Fenner said, 'Take it easy. I'll get a croaker.'

Nightingale shook his head. 'I got to talk,' he said hurriedly. 'No croaker can give me a new belly.' He bent forward slowly, pressing his forearms against his lower body.

'What happened?'

'I shot Thayler, and that rat Bugsey got me. I thought I could trust him. He put five slugs into me before I could shoot him. Then I fixed him all right.'

Fenner said, 'Why kill Thayler?'

Nightingale stared dully at the floor. When he spoke again his

131

voice was very thick. 'They killed Curly. That settled it. I wanted to get Carlos, too, but I guess I shan't now.'

'They killed her because you and she got me out of the fix.'

'Yeah, but Thayler always wanted her out of the way. She knew too much. She and me, we knew too much. We knew about you. Glorie was at the bottom of everything. She and her China-man.'

'What Chinaman?' Fenner asked softly.

'Chang. The guy they planted in your office.'

'You knew about that?'

Nightingale shut his eyes. He pressed his arms against his belly much harder. It was only by doing that, and by bending well forward, that he kept himself from falling apart. He said at last, in a faint, strangled voice, 'Yeah, I knew about it. Carlos found out about the Chink. Glorie was cheating with him. When Thayler took her to New York for a trip, Chang went along, too. That Chink did jobs for Carlos. Carlos thought he was fooling around with Glorie, so he sent a couple of guys to watch. They found out and they killed him. It was Thayler who had him moved to your office.'

Fenner stood very still, thinking, 'Why? Why to me, for God's sake?'

Nightingale shook his head. 'I don't know. He'd got some deep game.' He spoke slower, taking more pains to utter each word clearly. 'Something phoney happened on that New York trip. Something that started all this.'

'Chang? Was Glorie fond of him?' Fenner thought he was seeing an end to this business.

Nightingale shivered a little, but he wouldn't give up. Pain was eating into him and he was dying fast, but he pretended that he wasn't suffering. He wanted to show Fenner that he could take anything that was handed out without a squawk.

Nightingale said, 'She was crazy about him.' He began to sway a little in the chair.

'Where is she now?'

'She took it on the lam when the shooting started. Anyway, Thayler would have given her the heat if I hadn't broken in. I wish now . . . that . . . I'd've waited . . . before I shot him.'

Fenner was too late to catch him. He rolled off the chair on to the floor. Fenner knelt down and lifted his head. 'Crotti's a good guy,' Nightingale said faintly. 'You tell him I stood by you. That'll make things . . . even.' He peered up at Fenner through his thick lenses, tried to say something and couldn't quite make it.

Fenner said, 'I'll tell him. You've been a good guy to me.'

Nightingale whispered, 'Get after ... Carlos. He's got a dive ... back of Whiskey Joe's. ...'

He grinned at Fenner, then his face tightened and he died.

Fenner laid his head gently on the floor and stood up. He wiped his hands with his handkerchief, staring blankly at the opposite wall. Just Carlos now, he told himself, then maybe he'd get through with this business. As he put his handkerchief away he found the telegram. He pulled it out of his pocket and ripped the envelope. It ran:

Dead woman you thought Marian proved by finger prints to be kidnapped daughter of Andrew Lindsay. Suggest Marian not all she seems. Paula.

Fenner crumpled the cable slowly in his hand. 'So that's that,' he said. 'Now I guess I can finish this.'

He took one more look at Nightingale, then walked softly out of the bungalow.

Where was Glorie? Now Thayler was dead she was footloose again. Fenner thought he might find her with Noolen. She might, of course, have gone anywhere, but Noolen was worth trying. When a dame sees three men shot to death, and misses the same death by such a close margin, she's not likely to make smart plans. She had the skids under her, and she'd go to the one person left whom she knew well. She ought to know Noolen all right, Fenner argued. He was her husband, wasn't he?

He got back on the main street, hired himself a taxi, and went over to the Casino. Two patrolmen stood near the entrance, and they both gave him a hard look as he ran up the steps. Fenner grinned as he saw this evidence of Noolen's caution. He went through the big hall that was just closing down. Only one light burned, and apart from two Cubans in shirt-sleeves, covering the tables with dust-sheets, the hall was empty. They glanced up when Fenner came in.

'Noolen in still?' Fenner asked, heading for the office.

'He's busy right now,' one of the Cubans said, trying to intercept him. Fenner beat him to the door, pushed it open and went in.

Noolen, Kemerinski and Alex sat around the desk. A black

133

unlabelled bottle and glasses stood before them, and they all were smoking. They all looked up, their faces startled, then, seeing Fenner, they relaxed. Noolen scowled at him. 'What do you call this?' he said bitterly. 'Schaife and Scalfoni dead, and these two guys nearly shot to hell. This your idea of smashing Carlos?'

Fenner wasn't in the mood to play around with Noolen. He put his hands flat on the desk and looked Noolen in the face. 'Pipe down, you jerk. What've you got to bellyache about? Schaife and Scalfoni dead? So what? Think you can fight a war without any casualties. What about the other side? We've wiped out all their boats. We've burnt their base. Thayler's dead, Nightingale's dead, Miller's dead, Bugsey's dead, and six or seven others of the mob. Ain't that giving value for money?'

Noolen sat staring at him. 'Thayler?' His voice hardly reached above a whisper.

Fenner nodded. 'That leaves Carlos and Reiger. I particularly want those two guys myself. Then the gang's washed up.'

Kemerinski said, 'This guy knows what he's talkin' about. I'll play along with him still.'

Alex nodded and grunted.

Fenner said, 'Okay. What are we waitin' for? Where's Whiskey Joe's?'

'It's a joint near Nigger Beach.'

Fenner turned to Noolen. 'I'm goin' after Carlos. When I get back I've got something to say to you. Stick around. This is the finish of this business.'

He turned to the other two: 'Get a couple of Thompsons. We're goin' to Whiskey Joe's. Carlos's over there.'

Alex went away. Kemerinski said, 'Just we three?' He sounded a little uneasy.

Fenner shook his head. 'I'm going. You two come in later and clear up the mess.'

Fenner went out with Kemerinski. Alex was waiting in the car, nursing two Thompsons. As Kemerinski drove off, Fenner said, 'You two take the guns. You wait outside until you hear shooting, then come in and blast everything you see. Don't stop shooting until there's nothin' to shoot at – get it?'

Alex said, 'This has been a swell night.'

The big car went down Duval Street fast. Duval Street stretched right across the whole length of the island. It was late, and they met no cars. Kemerinski drove very fast. He cut speed as he reached South Street and swung the car to the right. At the bottom of South Street he drew to the kerb and killed the engine. 'Whiskey's over on the corner at Nigger Beach.'

Fenner got out of the car and began walking down the street. The other two followed him, holding the Thompsons under their coats.

Fenner said, 'He's got a place at the back. Would you know it?'

Alex said, 'There's a warehouse round the back, maybe that's it.'

'We'll go and look at it.'

Whiskey Joe's bar had closed for the night. It was just a small pile of black woodwork in the darkness. Alex said, 'Down this alley,' softly.

Fenner said, 'Stick around while I have a look. I'll be back.'

He went down the alley, which was very dark and smelt of decay and dark-alley smells. He walked carefully, not sneaking, but making no noise. At the end of the alley was a small square. Turning right and coming up behind Whiskey Joe's, he could make out a big square building with a flat roof. That, too, was a black silhouette against the star-filled sky. He got closer, found a door, tried it cautiously. It was locked. He moved along, looking for a window, turned the corner and worked his way along the south side. Still no windows. Round the next corner an iron ladder set close to the wall led upwards into the darkness. Fenner guessed it would take him on to the roof.

He went back fast and noiselessly to the other two waiting at the mouth of the alley. 'I think I've found the dump,' he said. 'There's only one door. All you two've got to do is to lie out there and start with the meat-grinder soon as they come out. Don't show yourselves, just lie flat and grind away.'

He could see Kemerinski's teeth as he grinned. 'I'll go up on the roof and send 'em out to you. Don't make mistakes, an' when you've done the job, beat it. I'll look after myself.'

The two grunted to show they understood, and then Fenner retraced his steps to the building. He climbed up the iron ladder, testing each rung before he put his weight on it. He counted forty rungs before he reached the top. As his head came over the balustrade he saw in the centre of the roof a square skylight, through which a light was shining.

Fenner knew that he'd have to be mighty careful how he crossed over. The slightest sound he made would be heard by anyone underneath. Before getting on to the roof he walked along the balustrade and looked over. He spotted Alex and Kemerinski hiding in a long ditch that was exactly opposite the door of the warehouse. They saw him and waved. He raised his hand, and then lowered himself from the balustrade to the roof.

Holding his gun in his right hand, he inched his way across the space that divided him from the skylight. It took him quite a time, but he did it without a sound. Pushing his hat to the back of his head he looked down into the room. Carlos was there. Reiger was there, and another man he didn't know. They were within six feet of Fenner. The room was very low, like a loft, and Fenner was so startled that he hurriedly jerked back.

Carlos was smoking on the bed. Reiger lolled, his head against the wall, in a chair; he was asleep. The other man dozed on the floor.

Fenner looked at the cross-pieces between the panes of the skylight; he felt their thickness gently with his thumb. There was no substance in them. Then he straightened and, reaching out with his right foot, he placed it gently in the exact centre of the cross-pieces. He took a deep breath and pushed down with all his weight.

The cross-pieces gave with a splintering noise and he and the glass crashed down into the room. He landed on his feet, staggered, and jerked up his gun.

Carlos lay very still on the bed, his cigarette jerking up and down in his mouth. The man on the floor went for his gun unconsciously. He was so dazed that his instinct took him to death. If he hadn't been dozing nothing on this earth would have made him go for the gun. Fenner shot him between the eyes.

Reiger and Carlos were like frozen statues. They just stared at Fenner with fixed glassy eyes.

Fenner said, 'I want you,' to Carlos.

The ash from Carlos's cigarette fell on to his chest. He looked wildly at Reiger and then back to Fenner. 'Gimme a break,' he said hoarsely.

Fenner said, 'Shut up. I've been layin' for you two. Now you're going to get what's coming to you. I'm not going to do it. You two guys can do it to yourselves. You can fight it out. The one who wins goes out of this joint. I won't touch him. Maybe you've heard I keep my word. Either that, or I'll knock the two of you off.'

Reiger relaxed suddenly. He said, 'I kill him and you don't touch me?' He sounded incredulous.

Carlos crouched further against the wall. 'Reiger!' he screamed. 'Don't do it! I'm your boss, do you hear? You're not to do it.'

Reiger got slowly out of his chair; he had a fixed grin on his face.

Fenner said, 'Wait. Put your mitts up and face the wall.'

Reiger scowled at him, but Fenner rammed his gun hard into his side. He put his hands up and turned round. Fenner took a gun out of his hip pocket and stepped back. 'Stay there an' don't move.' He went over to Carlos, grabbed him by his shirt-front, and dragged him off the bed. A quick frisk told him Carlos hadn't a gun.

Fenner walked to the corner of the room near the door and leaned against the wall. 'What you waiting for? Don't one of you want to go home?'

Carlos began to scream at Reiger, but the look on Reiger's face told him he'd have to fight. Reiger, his hands held low, a set animal expression on his face, began to stalk after Carlos, who circled the room swearing in a soft continuous flow. The room was too small to keep that up long. Reiger suddenly rushed in blindly, grabbing Carlos round the waist. Carlos screamed with terror, beat Reiger about his head with his clenched fists, and tried to get away. Reiger began to hit Carlos in the ribs, driving in punches that sounded hollow. They swayed round the room, punching and mauling each other, then Carlos's heel caught in the mat and he went over with Reiger on top of him. Reiger hammered his head on the boards. He turned his head and grinned at Fenner. 'I've got the louse now,' he panted. 'I've got him now!'

Carlos reached up with his hands and drove two hooked fingers into Reiger's eyes. A horrible sound issued from Reiger's chest and burst from his mouth in a sobbing croak. He fell away from Carlos. Holding one hand to his eyes and beating the air with the other, he began to blunder round the room. Carlos crawled to his feet, shook his head, and waited for Reiger to go past him again. As he did so, he shot out a foot and brought Reiger down. Reiger fell on his face and lay there, moaning and kicking with his feet.

Carlos had forgotten that Fenner was in the room. He saw only Reiger. Dropping on Reiger's back, he pinned him with his knees and fastened his red fingers round Reiger's throat. Reiger gurgled, groped feebly for Carlos's hands and then went limp. Carlos threw him away and stood up trembling.

Fenner leaned against the wall, covering Carlos with his gun. 'You're lucky,' he said. 'Beat it before I change my mind. Go on – dust, you –'

Carlos took two staggering steps to the door and flung it open. Fenner heard him blundering downstairs and he heard him fumbling at the lock. He stood, his head on one side, listening. Then out of the night came a sound of two Thompsons firing. Both gave a long burst, then there was silence.

Fenner put his gun away slowly and groped for a cigarette. 'I guess I've had about enough of this burg. I'll go home and take Paula out for a change,' he said to himself. He climbed out of the skylight and let himself down the iron ladder. As he did so he heard the sound of a car starting. It was Alex and Kemerinski calling it a day.

He went round and looked at Carlos. He had a tidy mind. He had had no doubt that those two would do a good job, but he liked to be sure. He need not have bothered. They'd done a good job.

He brushed down his clothes with his hand, thinking busily, then he turned and walked back towards Noolen's place.

Noolen started out of his chair when Fenner came in. He said, 'What happened?'

Fenner looked at him. 'What do you think? They're horse-flesh – both of them. Where's Glorie?'

Noolen wiped his face with his handkerchief. 'Dead? Both of them?' He couldn't believe it.

Fenner repeated impatiently, 'Where's Glorie?'

Noolen put two trembling hands on the desk. 'Why?'

'Where is she, damn you!' Fenner's eyes were intent and ice-cold.

Noolen pointed. 'She's upstairs. You can leave her out of this, Fenner. I'm goin' to look after her now.'

Fenner sneered. 'What's the idea? You're not falling for any line of repentance she's likely to hand out, are you?'

Noolen's face went a faint red. 'I don't want any cheap cracks from you,' he said. 'After all, she's my wife.'

Fenner pushed back his chair. 'For God's sake,' he said, getting to his feet, 'there's no fool like an old fool! Okay, if that's the way it stands.' He shrugged. 'Quite a dame, this Glorie. Off with the dead money-bags and on with the new.'

Noolen sat there, his hooded eyes fixed, and his mouth a little twisted. He said, 'Cut out your cracks, Fenner; I don't like them.'

Fenner turned to the door. 'I'm going to see that dame,' he said. 'Where shall I find her?'

Noolen shook his head. 'You ain't,' he said. 'Start somethin' here and you'll get a heap of grief.'

'So? Okay, then I don't see her; but I'll tell you what I'll do. I'll be back in an hour's time with the cops and a warrant for her arrest.'

Noolen sneered. 'You got nothing on that dame,' he said.

'Sure, I haven't. Only a murder rap. Still, what's a murder rap? Small change in your circle.'

Noolen's fat hands twitched, and his puffy face took on a greenish tinge. 'What are you talkin' about?' he said, with stiff lips.

Fenner moved to the door. 'You'll know. I haven't time to play around with you. I either see her now, or see her in jail. I don't give a damn which way it is.'

Noolen's face glistened in the light of the desk lamp. He said, 'Top door on the right upstairs.'

Fenner said, 'I won't be long, and you stay right where you are.' He went out and shut the door behind him.

When he got to the door on the right at the head of the stairs, he turned the handle and walked in. Glorie started up from a chair, her face white, and her mouth making a big O in her face.

Fenner shut the door and leaned against it. 'Keep your stockings up,' he said slowly. 'You and me are just going to have a little talk, that's all.'

She dropped back in the chair. 'Not now,' she said, her voice tight. 'It's late – I want to go to sleep ... I'm tired .. I told him downstairs not to let anyone up.'

Fenner selected a chair opposite her and sat down. He pushed his hat to the back of his head and dug in his vest-pocket for a packet of cigarettes. He shook two loose and offered them.

She said, 'Get out of here! Get out of here! I don't want –'

Fenner took one of the cigarettes and put the packet back in his pocket. He said, 'Shut up!' Then he lit the cigarette and blew a thin cloud of smoke up to the ceiling. 'You an' me are going to have a little talk. I'm talking first, then you are.'

She got out of the chair and started for the door, but Fenner reached out, caught her wrist, and pulled her round. She swung blindly for his face with hooked finger-nails. He caught her hand, imprisoned her two wrists in one hand and smacked her face with his other hand. Four red bars appeared on the side of her face, and she said, 'Oh!'

He let go of her hands and pushed her away roughly. 'Sit down and shut up!'

She sat down, her hand touching her cheek gently. She said, 'You're going to be sorry for that.'

Fenner eased himself in the chair so that it creaked. 'That's what you think,' he said, yawning. 'Let me tell you another little story. It'll slaughter you.'

She clenched her fists and pounded them on her knees. 'Stop! I know what you're going to say. I don't want to hear!'

Fenner said, 'For you there has never been anyone but Chang. When Carlos killed him, your life stopped. Nothing mattered to you. All you had to live for was to get even with Carlos for taking away the one thing that made your horrible life worth while. That's right, isn't it?'

She put her hands over her face and shivered, then she said, 'Yes.'

'Thayler and you went to New York for a short trip. You couldn't even be parted from Chang for a few days, so he came up and you saw him, when Thayler was busy elsewhere. Carlos sent two of his Cubans and they found Chang and killed him. That's right, too, isn't it?'

'They came in the night when I was with him,' she said. Her voice was expressionless. 'One of them held me while the other cut his throat. I was there when they did it. They said they'd kill me if he resisted, so he just lay on the bed and let that awful Cuban cut his throat. Somehow, he managed to smile at me when he was doing it. Oh, if you could have been there! If you could have seen him lying there with the Cuban bending over him. The sudden look of terror and pain in his eyes as he died! I could do nothing, but I swore that I'd get Carlos, I would smash everything he had built up.'

Fenner yawned again. He was feeling tired. 'You're not very nice,' he said. 'I can't feel any pity for you, because you always thought of yourself first. If you were really fine you would have had your revenge, even if it brought you down, too, but you hadn't the guts to lose what you already had, so you had to plot and plan to keep Thayler and get Carlos thrown to the wolves.'

Glorie began to cry.

Fenner went on, 'While this was going on, Thayler had found

himself a new toy. Thayler was a nasty bit of work, too. There was a girl called Lindsay. Maybe he met her at a party. He liked her and somehow he got her to go to his house. He knew you weren't about and he persuaded her to drop in. I can guess what happened. He tried to make her, but she fought him. That's how she got bruised, huh?'

Glorie went on crying.

'Well, he overdid it, didn't he? She died. When you got home, after Chang had been killed, you found Thayler running in circles with a corpse on his hands. That's the way it went, isn't it?'

'Yes.' She put her handkerchief to her eyes and began to rock herself backwards and forwards.

'You found the Lindsay dame dead, and her body badly bruised. Now, baby, it's your turn. Shoot! What did you do?'

Glorie said, 'You know all about it. Why ask me?'

'But why did you come to me?'

'I heard about you. I thought I saw my chance of saving Harry and starting trouble for Carlos. I heard you were tough and wouldn't stop at anything. I got a black wig, and wore simple clothes and came to you. I thought if –'

'You came to me as Marian Daley. You said your sister was missing. You thought if I took up the case I'd start eventually on Carlos. You gave me the hint. You said twelve Chinamen, because they always ship Chinamen over in dozens from Cuba, and I'd be smart enough to see that that was Carlos's racket. You planned with Thayler to have the Lindsay dame's body, without arms or legs or head, planted somewhere where I could find it, and I'd think that it was the body of Marian Daley. Since Marian never existed, Thayler couldn't be tried for killing a nonexistent person. So you tried to establish an identity between Marian and the body. To do this you got Thayler to fake up marks on your back, and when you came to see me he telephoned to give you an excuse for undressing. I saw the marks, and naturally enough they impressed me. It was a rotten plan, and it could never have held water in a court of law, but you might have confused the issue if you'd have played your cards right. But Thayler made mistakes.

'He wanted to get the body cut up and taken away from his house. He wanted to get your identity established with me as quickly as possible, otherwise the fact that the body, when found, could have proved that it couldn't have been yours from a doctor's evidence of time of death. First, you had to see me, then I was to be held up for a day or so, to give him time to set the stage the way he wanted. To hold me up, he planted Chang on me You didn't know this. He got his Cubans to take Chang along and put him in my office, hoping that the cops would come up and hold me for questioning. I beat him to it, found out where the Cubans came from, got there, killed them before they could get rid of one of the hands and arms of the Lindsay dame. By slipping up like that, he made a complete mess of things. That's the way it went, isn't it?'

Glorie sat limply in the chair. She said, 'Yes, that's right. It was a mad idea, but Harry was so scared he'd have done anything I told him to. I hadn't much time to make plans, but I thought it was an opportunity to get Carlos. I shook Harry down for ten grand. I gave you six, because I knew then that you'd follow up the case. I forged the letter giving you the necessary clues and then, when your secretary took me to the hotel, I waited my opportunity and ran away. That was the end of Marian Daley. I went back to Key West with Harry and waited for you to come. Thayler had told the Cubans to leave the body and the clothes at the Grand Central in a trunk. We were going to give you a tip so that you could have found them. I left that to Harry, but he messed it.'

Fenner lay back in his chair and stared at the ceiling. 'It was cock-eyed,' he said. 'If you'd've come to see me and told me about Carlos, I'd have gone for him just the same. A guy who handles people the way he did deserves all he gets.'

Glorie sat up very straight. 'You talk as if he's dead,' she said.

Fenner looked at her. 'He's dead all right. You're lucky. Seems like you've always managed to find a sucker to do your dirty work. Anyway, it was nice to see him go.'

Glorie drew in a long shuddering breath. She started to say something, but Fenner interrupted. 'The guy who killed Lindsay's daughter is dead. You're still my client. The Lindsay business is for the cops to work out. Maybe they'll find out about Thayler. Maybe they'll even get a line on you, but I'm not helping them. As far as I'm concerned, I'm through. You can link up with Noolen and go with him as fast as you like. I don't like you, baby, an' I don't like Noolen. I'll be glad to get back home. Whatever happens to you means nothing to me. You can be sure something will happen to you. A jane with your outlook can't last long. I'll leave it like that.'

He got up and wandered to the door, then, without looking back, he went out of the room.

Noolen was standing in the hall, staring up, as he walked down the stairs. He didn't even bother to look at him. Out in the street he took a deep breath, pulled at his nose thoughtfully, then set off at a fast pace in the direction of the Pan-American Airport.

SOME PANTHER AUTHORS

Norman Mailer
Jean-Paul Sartre
Len Deighton
Henry Miller
Georgette Heyer
Mordecai Richler
Gerard de Nerval
James Hadley Chase
Juvenal
Violette Leduc
Agnar Mykle
Isaac Asimov
Doris Lessing
Ivan Turgenev
Maureen Duffy
Nicholas Monsarrat
Fernando Henriques
B. S. Johnson
Edmund Wilson
Olivia Manning
Julian Mitchell
Christopher Hill

Robert Musil
Ivy Compton-Burnett
Chester Himes
Chaucer
Alan Williams
Oscar Lewis
Jean Genet
H. P. Lovecraft
Anthony Trollope
Robert van Gulik
Louis Auchincloss
Vladimir Nabokov
Colin Spencer
Alex Comfort
John Barth
Rachel Carson
Simon Raven
Roger Peyrefitte
J. G. Ballard
Mary McCarthy
Kurt Vonnegut
Alexis Lykiard